Heart-jacked

Messy Hearts #1

Charity Parkerson

Punk & Sissy Publications

Copyright

--Warning: This book is intended for readers over the age of 18.

Editor: Hercules Editing & Consultants

Photographer: FuriousFotog with cover model Golden Czermak

ISBN: 978-1-946099-66-2

Contents

Introduction

Two men with nothing in common. An instant connection neither man expects. It's an obsession born.

When his car gets recalled, River dreads a day wasted at the dealership. The sexy and overly helpful mechanic in charge of his car has him feeling a little better about the inconvenience. When his Mr. Fix-it, Nash, offers to do some extra work on River's car after hours for free, River can't pass up the deal. He never expects Nash to be kind, funny, and overwhelming. River definitely never expects Nash to steal his heart.

Even as Nash hears himself offer to work on River's car for free, he has no idea what's gotten into him. River is a tiny thing who looks skittish and entirely too breakable. Nash has never been accused of being any of those things. He's big, rough around the edges, and terrible at picking up men. No one is more surprised than Nash at how easily and quickly he finds his heart snagged by the guileless River. He'll do anything to make River his, even if it means upending his own life.

When two men from different worlds find themselves on common ground, both will have to find the strength to face their pasts if they hope to be together. Otherwise, they might miss a real shot at love.

Heart-jacked is the first book in bestselling author Charity Parkerson's Messy Hearts series. Messy Hearts is a series about imperfect men with messy lives who find something beautiful with their other halves. Hopefully, you'll find a couple to love.

Chapter One

THE FOUR WALLS OF the waiting room were covered in car advertisements. A complimentary coffee pot sat looking lonely next to packages of different-flavored creamers. River had long past memorized every detail, including the tiny crack in the wall that was poorly hidden. It was like they kind of wanted their customers to be happy but knew nothing about happiness themselves. The same guy had gotten up three times to look at the snacks but still hadn't picked one. River wondered if he was self-conscious about eating in public or just fidgeting. Either way, the middle-aged bald guy was the only entertainment River had, so he kept watching.

Dealing with a car recall was the last thing River wanted to be doing with his Saturday morning, but—sometimes—being an adult sucked, and it was better than missing a day of work. He had to put on his big boy pants and deal with it. No one would do this for him. That was what they should really be teaching in school. There should be a class where teenagers spend every day doing a different bullshit chore while panicking over how much it might end up costing. Even though a recall notice meant a free fix, they always found something else that needed to be done. Every damn time.

Honestly, River hadn't been waiting at the dealership for a horribly long time, but he was uncomfortable and out of his element. That made his time there feel like forever. It wasn't that River was an introvert or anything like that. It was just that—sometimes—he felt like everyone's eyes were on him. The sensation made him nervous and self-conscious. It was possible he suffered from a bit of anxiety. Today was definitely one of those days. He wanted to go home. By the time he heard his name called, River nearly leapt from his chair. They couldn't get him out of here fast enough.

"Yep. That's me."

A set of sweet-looking amber-colored eyes fixated upon River as he crossed the room. The closer River got, the bigger the guy became until River had to tilt his chin up to stay fascinated by those gorgeous eyes. Truth be told, the guy was a bit terrifying. Even though he wore the usual dark blue pants and shirt of a mechanic, River could picture the man in flannel and swinging an ax. He looked exactly like a lumberjack. River clenched his back teeth to stop the nervous chuckle rising in his throat from falling from his lips. His gaze dropped to the name tag stitched on the guy's shirt. Nash. That was oddly fitting. Someone named Nash should definitely have this guy's thick beard and massive arms.

"You need a new cabin air filter."

River blinked. "Is that a real thing?"

A smile exploded across Nash's face. It was heart-stopping. River automatically pressed his hand to his stomach. Nash's gaze dropped subtly before coming back to his. "Yes. It's a real thing. It keeps the dust, pollen, and smog from entering the air inside your vehicle. Yours is in bad shape and you shouldn't be breathing dirty air."

Oh. That made sense. "How much does that cost?"

Nash turned the small laptop he held River's way as if all the answers were right there. "It's a hundred and five if you have it done here." River nodded along while staring at the screen like he had any clue what he was looking at. "You could do it yourself, though, for like fifteen bucks. It's really easy to change. In fact, you can probably find a how-to video online."

River rocked from one foot to the other. He didn't really have an extra hundred bucks to throw around today, but it would end up costing a thousand if he tried doing it himself. He chewed his bottom lip and tried to decide what to do. "Um, is there any way it can wait? I'm not very handy and I don't get paid until next week.

And while fifteen bucks sounds great, I can't be trusted to work on machines of any kind."

Nash eyed him for a moment before casting a quick look around. When he met River's gaze again, River had to take a breath. Nash was uncomfortably hot. "If I wrote down the part number, could you pick it up from an auto parts store?"

Confusion had River drawing out his words. "I suppose I could."

"Good. You pick it up and I'll stop by tonight and pop it in for free."

River had nothing. Truly. He didn't know where to go with that. "Why?" God help him. The question just popped out. Nothing was ever free.

Nash shrugged. "You need it and I'm in the position to help. It seriously only takes like five minutes."

"Maybe there is something I can do for you in return." The offer jumped out so fast, River didn't have time to stop it before he realized how his words sounded. A soft and sexy-sounding chuckle fell from Nash's lips as River scrambled to fix his mistake. "That came out wrong. Jesus. I'd say I'm not always this dumb, but that would be a lie."

Nash's laughter died away. "Don't call yourself dumb. I understood what you meant." Nash glanced around again—like ensuring he was still safe to have this conversation. "Is the address listed on file still correct?"

"Yes."

"I'll leave a printout in your car of the part you need. Just take that to any auto parts store and they'll help you out. I'll be over around six, if that's good with you?"

An odd flutter of excitement went through River. "Six is great."

Nash gave him a sharp nod. "Cool. See you then. Otherwise, you're good to go. Your keys are in the ignition."

River bit his bottom lip to keep from smiling too much as he watched Nash walk away. He had a really great full ass. Nash made River feel tiny. River was, but dang. Nash was huge. River wanted to curl up in his arms. River shook his head and turned away. His thoughts were ridiculous. Nash had only offered to help pop a new filter in River's car. That was it. Nothing more. River always let his imagination get carried away. He needed to learn to stick to reality. River wasn't anything special. He didn't capture the attention of men the way other guys did. He was skinny and awkward. River didn't know how to flirt and didn't go out of his way to meet anyone. He was just some guy in a long line of men with nothing to offer at all. Someday, he would stop fantasizing about being swept off his feet. As he headed out to claim his car, River accepted he probably wouldn't stop dreaming today. Nash looked damn sexy in his uniform. Maybe it couldn't hurt to fantasize a little. It wasn't like anyone would ever know.

Goddamn. That was really all Nash could think. He still couldn't believe he had risked his job to make that offer. Nash couldn't explain his recklessness. One second, he had been talking about one thing while River had stared up at him with those huge blue eyes. The guy had freckles across the bridge of his nose. He looked innocent and shy. Nash was a sucker for all of that. Then River had blushed. Goddamn. The curse wouldn't stop overtaking Nash's mind. Nash had to help him out. The boy needed a man. Nash had time.

"Hey, Nash. Your brother is here."

Nash suppressed a groan at the called words. He nodded Tracy's way, letting her know he had heard before heading out the bay door to meet his brother. Jason usually only stopped by when he wanted something. Nash was never in the mood for that.

Jason smiled and straightened away from his Harley when he spotted Nash. He was the epitome of good looks. Blond and fit. He looked exactly like his dad, Nash's stepfather. Nash and Jason looked nothing alike. In fact, people never believed them when they said they were related. Unless they were in trouble, then everyone knew they were kin. "Hey, big brother." Big brother? Fantastic. He wanted something for sure.

"What's up?"

Jason's smile faltered at Nash's less than welcoming tone. "I just wanted to see if you were free after work. Maybe we can hit Roadie's Bar?"

Nash shook his head. "Sorry. I have a side job tonight."

Jason curled his nose. "On a Saturday night? Dude. You need to go out. Have fun. Get laid.

There's always a surplus of hot chicks at Roadie's."

First off, no, there wasn't. Secondly, he preferred the company of men. Not that Jason knew enough about Nash to know that. In conclusion, he wasn't interested. Nash shrugged. "Money first."

"Yeah, I can see that." Jason swiped his palms on his thighs. His expression turned uncomfortable. "Actually, speaking of which, I was wondering if there was any way you could help me out this month. Things at work have been slow, and you know..."

Nash kept his expression blank by pure willpower alone. The thing was, Jason was his brother and Nash knew he genuinely needed the help, but fuck. Jason had been needing help for a long time, and he wasn't trying to change his circumstances. He just kept coming to Nash instead of looking for a different job or staying home on the weekends until things picked up. Nash was tired of helping. He loved his brother. Nash just couldn't carry him forever.

Jason looked crestfallen. "I know you're tired of me. It's just that rent is due, and Dad couldn't make payroll this week if he paid me."

Nash's eye twitched. He exploded. "Are you fucking kidding me, Jason? Why do you keep doing this? People aren't supposed to pay who they want and fuck the rest. You need to start looking out for yourself. Mike obviously doesn't give a shit if you make it, so why do you give a fuck if he does? That's your money. You worked for it."

"He's my dad," Jason shot back. "Just because you're not loyal to the family doesn't mean I'm not. Plus, it's not like the money is strictly legal, so who can I complain to?"

"Not loyal? If I'm so damn disloyal, then why am I the only one supporting you? Also, that's not my fucking dad. That's yours. I don't owe him shit."

Jason made a sweeping gesture towards the dealership. "Don't owe him shit? Who taught you all this? You wouldn't have a job either if it wasn't for Dad. He's the one who gave you the skills to walk away from him."

"It's a good goddamn thing I did walk away," Nash said, refusing to back down. "Otherwise, you wouldn't have anywhere to turn when he fucks you."

Jason's shoulders fell. He swiped his hand down his face before focusing on Nash again. "Look, you know I didn't mean any of that. I'm just upset and tired of being broke. I'll go take out a title loan against my bike or whatever."

Guilt sneaked in. Jason was just dumb enough to lose his bike on a nothing loan from a crooked title dealer. "How much do you need?"

"A thousand."

The red was back, coating Nash's vision. "Holy shit, Jason. Do you really think I have a thousand dollars just sitting around to give to you, especially since I know you'll never pay me back? Even if Mike does pay you later, you'll blow it on some bullshit without another thought to me. The way you always do."

Jason's gaze skirted away. "Like I said, don't worry over it. I'll figure it out. It was good seeing you." He straddled his Harley and fired it to life before Nash could decide what to do. Nash watched with his heart in his throat as Jason drove away. His chest hurt. He never knew how such a shitty family always made him feel like the bad guy.

With a growl, Nash dug his phone out and sent Jason the money through a cash app. At the end of the day, Jason was his baby brother and he couldn't let him be homeless. That didn't mean he had to be silent.

Nash: *How fucking dare you not pay Jason the paycheck he's earned? You're a piece of shit. You've always been a piece of shit. And because I'm the ungrateful asshole, I know you're about to call me, I added Mom to this text exchange.*

Mom: *What? Wait. You didn't pay Jason? What the hell?*

Mike: *I removed your mom from this discussion. You're right, you are an ungrateful asshole. Without me, you wouldn't have a goddamn thing. Jason understands why I couldn't pay him this week. You need to stay out of family business. You're no longer a part of this one.*

Nash: *Good.*

While eating up the parking lot with his long stride, Nash shoved his phone back in his pocket. He had work to do. God knew someone needed to be making some money, and—apparently—he was the only one capable of supporting anyone. Before he made it back inside, he spotted River's blue Nissan Altima still sitting in the parking lot. Nash changed directions when he realized River sat behind the wheel. River never looked up from whatever he stared at in his lap. Nash tapped his knuckles on the driver's side window. River jumped and rolled down the window, patting his chest.

A smile washed over Nash. "Sorry. I didn't mean to startle you. Is everything okay?"

Big blue eyes stared up at him from inside the car. His shitty day washed away as River smiled. A dark lock of hair fell across his eye. Nash automatically pushed it behind River's ear. He shoved his hands in his pockets when he realized what he had done. River never stopped smiling.

"I'm good. I was just reading the paperwork, looking at everything that was done to the car. It's crazy the small things you never think about until you get a recall notice."

Nash nodded. "Everything is computerized nowadays. At least you know you bought a car from a company that cares about your safety."

"True. My dad used to work for the company and now he won't buy anything else. I guess that stuck with me when it came time to buy a new car." His gaze moved over Nash's face, as if searching for something in his expression. "Are you okay?"

Nash wasn't one to smile a lot. Mostly, that was due to not having anything to smile about, but he forced his features into something resembling a smile for River. "Yeah. I just spotted you out here and worried you had run into a problem."

"Nah." River chuckled. The sound had Nash taking a breath. "Truthfully, I'm always slow. I don't know why. It drives everyone crazy."

Nash shrugged. “As long as you’re okay.” Nash took a step back, easing toward the door, even though he didn’t want to leave River’s company for some reason even he couldn’t explain. “So, I’ll see you at six.”

Humor flashed in River’s eyes. “Six.”

“I should get back to work.”

“You probably should.”

Nash nodded. “Until six, then.”

River laughed and rolled up his window. Nash couldn’t stop smiling as he turned away. The whole day hadn’t been complete shit, and it wasn’t over yet. Pretty soon he would be alone with his adorable new friend. That was something worth looking forward to. He wouldn’t let Mike’s bullshit ruin his day. Like the man had said, Nash wasn’t family anymore.

HEART-JACKED

Chapter Two

It had taken River all the way until fifteen minutes before six for realization to hit. He had invited a complete stranger to his home. Nash could be a rapist or a serial killer. As quickly as the worry struck, it was gone. River might not have a lot going for him, but he was a good judge of character. His sixth sense about people had served him well over the years. Plus, he would not spend his life in fear. The only way to make new friends was to put everything out there. Inviting a stranger to his home definitely fit that bill. Plus, despite being huge, Nash looked kind of sweet. River was oddly excited to see him again.

Still, even once he pushed the worry from his mind, River's heart tried leaping from his chest when the knock came. He answered the door to find the same butterflies in his stomach as the first time they had spoken. Nash looked like a warrior. His work shirt was gone. In its place was a white tank top that showed off his tattooed muscles. The Florida heat had a fine sheen of sweat glistening on his darkly tanned skin. River had to force his gaze to stay locked on Nash's face as he stepped outside, joining Nash on the porch.

"Hi."

Nash didn't return his greeting. His amber gaze traveled down River's body, openly inspecting him. River's skin heated every place Nash's stare touched. He fought the urge to rush to his bedroom and put on more clothes.

"Get your shoes on."

River came back to himself at the order. "What?"

Nash met his gaze. "Get your shoes on. You're going to change this filter so you know how to do it next time. There are a lot of small things you should know how to do yourself so no one can take advantage of you."

There was a small part of River that was insulted—like Nash had just called him inept or something. Another, bigger slice of River was moved. He felt kind of funny. It was like he was being protected. "Okay."

Without asking permission, Nash followed him inside. He hovered in the doorway, watching as River stamped into a pair of shoes without unlacing them. When the tongue of his left shoe bunched at the top of his foot, River bent and tugged it out again. When he straightened, River's breath caught. Nash didn't hide the way his eyes followed River's every move. He didn't smirk or leer. His face was free of all emotion. The strangest sensation washed over River. He felt cherished and safe. He shook his head, trying to dispel his odd thoughts. They didn't know each other and likely never would. Nash probably had a wife and three kids waiting at home. Since River looked like no more than a kid himself, Nash was probably having a fatherly moment. River forced himself to smile and head for the door.

"Just tell me what I need to do."

Nash pulled a screwdriver from his back pocket. "It's inside the glovebox."

With a nod, River grabbed the bag with the filter inside and headed out to the car. He opened the passenger side door and dropped the bag in the seat before opening the glove box. "Okay. I can do this." Honestly, he didn't think he could do this.

Nash passed him the screwdriver. "If you look inside, you'll see a small panel. Unscrew the screws and pop it open."

While suppressing a tired sigh, River dove in. He had zero interest in learning how to work on his car. River understood Nash's point, though. It would be kind of nice if he wasn't a complete idiot when it came to his car. He was tired of the dealership trying to sell him expensive maintenance every time he got his oil changed. Maybe he would learn something today. It couldn't hurt to try.

Watching River's ass in tiny shorts and bent over inside his car made Nash feel like a pervert. He tried looking everywhere but at the sexy round ass that bounced around in the air at the perfect height to get fucked. Seriously, all Nash had to do was take three steps and he could close the space between them. The temptation was crippling and bordered on creepy. He had the best of intentions. Truly. Nash hadn't come here to molest the man. He just hadn't expected River to answer the door dressed like a snack. Nash didn't think it was purposeful. He didn't believe River tried to tempt him. It was a typical Florida summer. Hot as fuck. That required hot as fuck clothing decisions. Goddamn, though. Yum.

River glanced over his shoulder. "Okay. What now?"

Nash tore his hungry gaze away from River's ass and focused on his face. Big blue eyes stared back at him. Nash took a slow breath. River needed someone to take care of him, Nash reminded himself. That was why he was here. He forced his attention on his task and walked River through changing the filter, step by step. He did great. Nash never had to step in and help. When River closed the passenger side door and turned Nash's way wearing a bright smile, his open pride stirred something in Nash's chest.

"I did it."

A smile tugged at Nash's lips. "You did. Now you never have to depend on anyone else to do that for you. Next time, we'll change your windshield wipers."

River visibly tried and failed to suppress his smile. "Next time?"

River's hopeful tone had Nash's smile growing. He didn't repeat himself. They both knew there would be a next time.

A hint of a blush touched River's cheeks. He rolled Nash's screwdriver between his hands. "Um. I know you offered to come by for free, but can I repay you with dinner? I've had a roast slow-cooking all day. It's way too much food for one person."

Nash's stomach growled. It had nothing to do with food. "I'd like that."

With a sharp nod, River headed for the house before stopping just as quickly and turning Nash's way. "Oh, here." He handed back Nash's screwdriver. Nash moved to stash it in the saddlebag on his Harley. He was bad about stuffing tools in his back pocket and forgetting them. He didn't want to do that tonight. Nash already planned to have his mind on other things.

"Nice bike," River said behind him. "Not that I have anything to compare it to," he tacked on nervously.

"I take it you've never ridden."

"I've never done a lot of things." The laughter in River's voice had Nash's gaze locked on him, searching for every drop of happiness in his expression. River bled innocence. It was oddly fascinating to Nash. He was obviously a grown man but untainted by life. A need to protect

River grew by the second in his company. The world was an ugly place.

“Go put some jeans on and I’ll take you for a ride.” The offer was out there before he considered it. He didn’t have a helmet for River, and he wasn’t taking the guy anywhere without a helmet.

River shook his head. “No thank you. Maybe someday I’ll be braver, but I’m not really. Brave, that is,” he said, clarifying his statement with a wince.

Nash got it. He wouldn’t push. “If you ever change your mind, I’m the guy to call.”

River cocked his head slightly and stared at Nash in a way he couldn’t explain, but River’s expression stirred something in his chest. It was like he was seen for the first time in years. While dozens of people looked at him and interacted with him every day for various reasons, no one actually saw him. River saw him.

"You're the guy everyone calls, aren't you? Like, hey, my car broke down. Can you stop by after work? My girl dumped me today. Can we get a beer? I don't have any food. Can I borrow ten bucks?" River pitched his voice to different tones with each question. By the time he was done, Nash couldn't stop smiling, despite how the words punched him in the chest while hitting too close to home.

"It's like you've been spying on me. That's exactly my life."

"Ha. My streak of reading people continues with you." River headed for the door looking triumphant. Nash followed on his heels while smiling like an idiot.

"What about you?" Nash asked as they stepped inside and toed off their shoes by the door. "Which guy are you?" He cast a quick glance around the living room as he posed the question. It was a nice place in an upper end neighborhood. His curiosity doubled. River drove a new car and had a nice house. Yet he was young and seemed to live alone. Everything in his living room looked moderately expensive and clean.

River didn't seem to notice Nash inspecting his place. He closed the door behind them and kept up his end of the conversation. "I'm the River-will-take-care-of-it guy," River said, waving for Nash to follow him. They moved to the kitchen. It smelled like heaven. The scent of cooking food lingered in the air. Nash fought the urge to lift the lid from the crockpot and sneak a peek. River headed for the sink to wash his hands. He spoke over his shoulder. "You know, Granny needs to go to the doctor. River will take her. There's a repairman coming sometime between seven a.m. and midnight. Call River. He'll spend the entire day waiting for them. I need someone to keep the cats next week while I'm on vacation. River will do it. It doesn't matter he's allergic to cats. He never says no to anything."

There was a hint of bitterness in that speech. Nash got it. He was resentful as hell over everyone always calling him to fix everything. "You should definitely say no now and then. It's good for the soul."

River shrugged as he dried his hands. A sad smile passed over his lips. "I guess if I'm not the person who never says no, then I would be the guy no one ever calls at all. So, really, which is worse?"

"One hundred percent the guy who never says no," Nash said with a laugh.

River's eyes danced with laughter. "You must have siblings. Only someone inundated with brothers and sisters would prefer the silence." His humor disappeared. "Or a house full of kids."

Nash snorted. "No kids." He moved to wash his hands too. The soap smelled so strong of cherries that Nash lifted the bottle to check out the brand as he spoke. "I do have siblings. A younger brother and several stepbrothers. I was the quiet middle child with a different mom from everyone older and a different dad than my younger brother. The odd man out," Nash said absently as he dried his hands. He tossed his paper towel in the trash before meeting River's stare again. "This is a really nice place. What do you do for a living?"

"I work for Serenity Concepts. It's a high-end spa where people get anything from lipo to Botox to a manicure and massage. I'm a cosmetologist there. I do hair. Give facials. That sort of thing."

"It sounds like you deal with a lot of assholes all day."

A sexy laugh escaped River. "I really do, but I also have a lot of regulars who are super nice. It balances itself out."

Nash cast another look around the room. The floors were hardwood and the kitchen table looked to be solid oak. The refrigerator probably cost as much as a used car. "It seems like I got into the wrong business."

River pulled a face as he opened a nearby cabinet and pulled out two plates. "I wish I could claim I did all this on my own. I should admit; my mom owns Serenity Concepts. She handles all the surgical procedures there."

"Your mom is a surgeon?"

River nodded. "And I'm her only child, so I'm pretty spoiled." He scooped a huge helping of roast, carrots, and potatoes onto a plate before adding some cornbread to the side. After digging forks from the drawer, River passed the plate Nash's way and kept talking. "There's water in the fridge. I always knew I wanted to make people pretty the way my mom does, but I also knew I wasn't cut out to be a doctor. Mom let me start working at the spa when I was fourteen, and I did little things—like sweeping or sanitizing the manicure sets. I worked my way up and earned my degree on the side. While she's always made me earn my keep—for the most part—she's also a great mom. She won't let me go without." He motioned around him. "So I can't really claim I did this by myself." River fixed a much smaller plate for himself, switched the crockpot to warm, and then moved to the kitchen table.

After grabbing two bottles of water from the fridge, Nash followed. They sat side by side. The meat was so tender, it was falling apart while Nash scooped a bite into his mouth. He damn near moaned in delight. While he could cook, this was different. River was obviously a gift from God. "This is otherworldly."

River beamed at the compliment. “It’s my grandmother’s recipe. Hence the always being the one who takes her to the doctor,” he added with a chuckle.

“Definitely worth it.” He bit into the cornbread. It was sweet just like his grandmother used to make. Nash was pretty sure he should just marry River right then. Even if he turned out to be a horrible person, Nash wouldn’t go hungry. He swallowed his food. “If I hang around too long, you’ll have to roll me out the door, but I’m coming over every night if you always cook like this. I’ll be even fatter by Christmas.”

River slapped his arm. “You’re not fat. Jesus. But you are more than welcome to join me for dinner anytime you want. It’s nice to not eat alone for once.”

Nash couldn't agree more. He had been eating alone for so long that most nights he didn't think about it at all. It was the nights he did think about it that really got to him. "That sounds nice. I'll buy the groceries if you cook."

River had the sweetest smile. Nash couldn't look away from it. "You're nice. I wasn't sure what to expect tonight."

"Me either, but I'm glad I came." River had no idea how much Nash meant those words. Life had been kind of shitty for a long time now. He wasn't one for the hookup culture and he wasn't the typical type of guy everyone seemed to want. He wasn't skinny and bubbly. Nash had always had a large frame and lots of muscle, but he wasn't a gym rat. It was more genetics that would go to full-on fat if he let it. Nash had always fantasized that he would meet someone in the grocery store while reaching for the same six pack of beer or whatever—like fate would find him where he stood someday. His gaze slid River's way. Maybe it finally had. He was willing to find out.

No matter how hard he tried, River couldn't stop his eyes from turning Nash's way. He was impossible to ignore. River fought a crazy urge to curl up in the man's lap and snuggle. He forced himself to focus on other things—like getting to know Nash.

"What about you? How long have you been a mechanic?"

"Practically all my life," Nash answered between bites. "My dad was a mechanic. Mom says he gave me a wrench to play with as a toddler. I don't remember him, really. From my mom's stories, I know he was from Thailand and that's how I ended up with this gorgeous year-round tan." Nash flashed him a smile filled with humor. It slipped away as he continued. "There's this snapshot in my head of sitting in his lap and eating fries from his plate, but I'm not sure if it's real. He died when I was two. My mom remarried almost immediately and had my brother not long after. I think she was too broken-hearted to be alone." River made a sympathetic noise. He couldn't imagine losing his dad. Nash kept talking, saving River from having to find the right words. "My stepdad, Mike, owns a motorcycle repair shop and is a complete ass. But my mom seems pretty determined not to leave the situation, so I just got out as quick as possible to get out of the way. I took some auto mechanics classes at night and worked at the dealership during the day, changing oil and whatnot. When I kept fixing things better and faster than the guys with degrees, they moved me to full-time mechanic. I quit the night classes and jumped in. I've been there twelve years now, I guess."

"Twelve years. That's awesome. It sounds like you're happy there. How old are you?" River fought a blush. He tried to be tactful, but the question didn't come out sounding that way. River sounded like he dug for info.

If Nash noticed, he didn't show it. "I'm thirty-two. What about you?"

Relief washed over River. He wasn't alone in his questioning. "Twenty-four."

"Wow. You look eighteen." Nash nodded toward River's plate before River could decide if he was offended. "Are you finished? You cooked. I'll wash the dishes."

River's heart melted a little. He couldn't explain it. "Yes, but that's not necessary. We can just pop these in the dishwasher."

With a nod, Nash stood. He grabbed their plates and headed for the sink. As River looked on, he rinsed them before putting everything in the dishwasher. It hit River. He didn't want Nash to leave. Not yet.

River scrambled for an excuse for Nash to stay. "If your offer still stands, I'll go change and you can take me for a ride."

While drying his hands, Nash turned and focused on River. His expression gave nothing away as Nash's gaze swept over River. "Do you really want to go or are you hoping I'll stay?"

Despite River's immediate desire to deny the truth, he found himself being honest. "I'm hoping you'll stay."

Nash threw his paper towel away and helped himself to another bottle of water while River fought the urge to take back his confession.

River lost the battle against himself. "Never mind. It's Saturday and you probably have a life and—"

"What do you usually do on Saturday nights?" Nash asked, cutting his rambling short.

The urge to squirm doubled. "I'm pretty boring. Usually, I just find something to watch on TV and surf the web on my phone. I don't..." River massaged his arm, feeling exposed. He started to say he didn't have friends. The confession was too much, even for him.

Nash nodded toward the living room. "Let's find a movie to watch."

River bit his bottom lip, trying to hide how happy the suggestion made him. He grabbed a bottle of water and led the way. While Nash settled on the couch, River snagged the remote and joined him. He chose the opposite end.

Nash glanced his way. "You could sit a little closer."

It was getting harder not to smile like an idiot. He slid a little closer, moving to the center of the couch.

"I meant closer than that." He lifted his arm. River didn't miss his chance to slip beneath and snuggle against Nash's side. Nervous laughter rose in his throat. He swallowed it.

"There's a lever on the inside," River said, pointing to the arm of the couch.

Nash reached between the cushion and arm. The footstool popped out. He pushed, reclining his end of the couch. River found himself curled up in Nash's arms. Somehow, Nash ended up with the remote. He started flipping through channels while River hunted for the sound of his heartbeat. Once he found it and pressed his ear closer, River realized he probably looked like he was nuzzling the guy's massive chest. He was, but still. Nash landed on an animated kid's movie that was one of River's favorites. He hesitated and then moved on. Before River could voice his disappointment, Nash went back to the movie.

"I kind of like this one."

A smile exploded across River's face at Nash's embarrassed-sounding confession. "It's one of my favorites. Check the guide. I wonder if the second one is coming on next."

Nash pressed the button, making the guide appear. "Looks like it."

"Yay." River didn't care he sounded like a kid. He was happy. In fact, River would go as far as to say he hadn't felt like this in years. He was poised on the edge of his seat in his mind, waiting to see what happened next. Nothing new or thrilling ever happened to him. He snagged a nearby throw blanket and cuddled as close as he could get to Nash. Before he could get too comfortable, he felt Nash's muscles tense.

"Hold on." Nash shifted positions. His hand slid across River's throat before urging River's chin up until River met his gaze. "I need to get something out of the way." Before River could puzzle through Nash's claim, Nash kissed him. At first, it was a mere brushing of lips. A sweet promise. Then Nash dragged River higher up his body and claimed River's mouth. River was half sprawled across Nash's body while Nash explored his mouth. There was nothing sweet about the way their tongues roughly brushed. Nash bit River's bottom lip and sucked. All River could do was hang on for the ride.

His heartbeat pounded in his ears. River's body was on fire. He had never considered himself a sexual being. In fact, River would go as far as to say he had low to no sex drive. Until Nash's kiss, River hadn't known a person could go from nothing to damn near coming in their clothes in an instant. It was just that Nash was extremely manly. He messed with River's hormones. Nash's kiss softened until their lips barely brushed.

"I'd hoped I would stop fantasizing about kissing you if I did it." Nash kissed the tip of his nose, somehow making even that seem sexy while River's heart melted. "It didn't work. Now I want more." He didn't give River a chance to respond or catch his breath. Nash delved inside again, dominating their kiss. River thought he might burst into flames. He tried hard not to hump Nash's body like a horny dog. He forced his hands to stay still where they clung to Nash's chest. It was a nice spot to be, after all. His chest was solid muscle. It blew River's mind that someone so sexy wanted him. He refused to look a gift horse in the mouth. His heart beat so hard, River expected it to burst from his chest. River's body throbbed with lust. His head spun from the excitement. When Nash pulled away and kissed a path to River's ear, River fought for air.

Nash's lips stroked the spot beneath his earlobe. "You're killing me. Let's watch this movie before I'm too far gone to stop."

Even though River's body screamed in denial, River nodded and settled onto Nash's chest to watch the movie. He didn't see a thing. It was like the room had been plunged into murky water. A haze coated his vision while his mind raced. River fought for a distraction from his aching need. His mind came to the rescue with a million and one thoughts about the night. Damn. He really liked this one. It had been such an odd and unexpected day. River prayed Nash didn't turn out to be crazy or mean. Oh, God. Or a cheater. Please don't let him be that. River's brain hopped from one horrible scenario to the next. What if he left tonight and River never saw him again? At the thought, River stroked Nash's stomach, trying to get his caresses in before he lost his chance. His eyes fell closed in delight. There was a slight indention of abs. He forced his hand to be still before he made any more discoveries. He really, really liked this one.

The second movie started, making River realize how long he had been savoring Nash's heart beating against his ear. He needed to treat Nash like a guest and stop petting him. Maybe he should get snacks or something.

"Would you like..." River lifted his head. His words dried up as he caught sight of Nash.

With one arm draped over his eyes, he slept peacefully. A smile tugged at the corners of River's mouth. He had pet the man to sleep. River swallowed a chuckle and slipped from the couch. Poor Nash. He had worked all day and then come to help River. The guy was probably exhausted.

River draped the throw blanket over Nash, making sure he was covered. After switching off the TV, he stole another minute to stare at Nash. He was just so overwhelming and nice. Damn. It had been a long time since River had met anyone so kind. He would let the man sleep. As River turned out the lights, he caught himself brushing his fingers across his lips. They still tingled from Nash's biting kisses. It truly had been such an unexpected day. For the first time in a long time, River couldn't wait to see what happened next.

Chapter Three

THE HOUSE EVEN FELT empty without Nash. After showering and eating breakfast, River trailed from room to room, holding his coffee between his hands. It went cold while he fought the growing loneliness. He had gotten used to a quiet life. Then this huge mechanic with a sexy smile had shown up and filled a space River hadn't wanted to admit was empty. He couldn't say he loved being single. River simply wasn't very outgoing. Every day, he spent the entire day smiling and chatting with clients. By the time he got home, he didn't want to socialize anymore. He didn't want to go to clubs and pretend he wasn't trying to meet anyone. Plus, all those guys were just looking to fuck. River's mind drifted back to that kiss. His body immediately stirred. Maybe he kind of wanted that too.

River shook his head. He wanted more than a night of potentially disappointing sex with someone he would never see again. River liked kissing and snuggling. He wanted to fall in love. A growl sneaked out. He was alone and no one could hear his thoughts. Yet he still felt ridiculous for admitting he wanted something he wasn't sure existed any longer. Everyone was swiping right and meeting strangers from the internet. Never looking back. River wanted someone so familiar with his body that River didn't blush when they stripped him. He wanted something real.

With a sigh, he moved to the couch and sat where he had left Nash. The blanket he had draped over him was now neatly folded. It was like Nash had never been there. A hollow space opened in River's gut. He probably wouldn't see Nash again. It was stupid how much that thought hurt. In one night, Nash had felt... real. They had already felt comfortable to River—like a couple. Now he didn't even have Nash's number. He hadn't given Nash his. Things were just over—like a cruel taste of everything he would never have.

River set his coffee aside and dug for the handle to kick out the recliner. He wanted to settle into Nash's spot and cling to the last wisps of him. His hand collided with something smooth. River pulled. He stared at the object in surprise. It was a wallet. He flipped it open. Nash's picture stared back at him. A smile exploded across his face at the sight.

River looked closer, inspecting every feature. A sigh stuck in his throat. He was so yummy. That thick beard. Those eyes. Damn. River's gaze slid the date of birth. September second. He checked out the address. River blinked. He knew exactly where Nash lived. When he was a kid, his aunt had lived on that road. River remembered it well, because his best friend had also lived on the same street. He had spent every weekend walking between his best friend's house and his aunt's house. That was the craziest thing. It felt like a sign. He should take Nash his wallet. If it were River, he would be flipping out if his wallet went missing. It was the perfect excuse to see him. Get his number. River's smile grew. He would change first. Maybe he would only get a few minutes with Nash, but he should show his best assets. A squeal escaped him as he shot to his feet. He would get to see Nash again today. It felt like a win.

Since leaving River's, Nash felt off—like he was missing something. He should have waited until River was awake before he left. Nash realized too late he hadn't even gotten River's number. He told himself he would look it up at work tomorrow, but that wasn't enough. Nash kept remembering that kiss. Goddamn. He had forced himself to stop when River made a sound that damn near had Nash coming in his jeans. Maybe he could have convinced River to take him to bed, but then he might not have seen him again. Even though River didn't strike him as a one-night stand guy, Nash recognized he didn't know River. Not really. Yet, he felt like he did.

River was fantastic. He was an amazing cook and hadn't hesitated to watch ridiculous TV with him. River hadn't gotten upset and kicked Nash out when Nash's long day caught up with him. Nash didn't think their night together constituted a date, but it had been amazing. River fit perfectly in his arms and smelled like a dream. Nash's dick stirred as the image of River in those tiny shorts filled his mind. He shook his head, trying to dispel the fantasy of peeling the next-to-nothing material from River's body. Nash fired the shower to life and stripped. He had errands and shit today. He couldn't stand around dreaming all day. Maybe he would hit the grocery store and pick up some things for River—kind of building on their discussion of Nash buying the groceries if River cooked. He could show up at River's door and make the guy smile with his offering before taking him out to dinner. It was a thought. Any plan at all was better than thinking he would never see River again.

Nash stepped beneath the pounding stream of hot water. Butterflies stirred in his stomach the instant he closed his eyes and found River's image waiting there. Those big blue eyes. Jesus. Nash could see them looking up at him with River on his knees. He couldn't recall wanting anyone so badly so fast. Nash wasn't even one hundred percent certain what had snagged his attention so thoroughly, but he wanted River.

Nash had to take a breath. He flattened his palm against the shower wall as his knees weakened. That kiss. He swore it still lingered on his lips. River kissed like he wanted to get fucked. Nash had what he needed, but he didn't want to rush. He liked the way River watched him—like he didn't want Nash to leave. Nash adored the way River blushed, as if he felt Nash's hunger. He couldn't ignore the way his cock throbbed any longer. Nash palmed his erection. He would go see River again today. Nash needed to take the edge off just in case River let him stay again. They weren't there yet. River didn't need anyone to survive. He was too independent to keep Nash for anything. If he touched River now, he might not get to a second time.

Nash dropped his chin and sucked air as pleasure rippled through him. His hips rolled as he stroked, fucking his hand. Behind his closed eyes, River bent over the passenger seat again, ass up and wiggling as he tried changing the filter. Those tiny shorts had tempted Nash like he hadn't been tested in a long time. River's perfect shape had Nash wanting to peel those shorts down his legs and spread those cheeks. Except the idea had a hint of disappointment sinking in. The image changed in Nash's mind. River straddled his hips and stared down at Nash with those gorgeous eyes. Full lips parted and swollen from Nash's kiss. Nash audibly panted. He pumped faster, moving closer to the edge. Nash could picture his dark hands against River's pale skin as he guided River into the perfect pace. River looked so innocent and untouched—like he needed a protector. A teacher. Nash would make him happy.

A flash of longing hit as Nash's orgasm tore through him. He wanted River. Nash wanted to be inside him right then. He craved the sensation of River's body, sucking him dry as Nash teased him into orgasm. He missed being touched, but he missed being looked at the way River watched him even more. Nash squeezed out every drop of cum while the craving for River grew. He gasped, trying to catch his breath. Nash would go see River. He liked him and missed him already. It was insane, but Nash had never claimed to be cursed with sanity.

Nash rushed through getting dressed. He barely bothered brushing his hair. With an old t-shirt and ragged jeans covering him, he searched for his keys. Maybe he should take the truck today. He had let River cook last night. Nash should take him out tonight. It sucked that he had given

Jason so much money—thanklessly—since that limited how much he could do for River.

The doorbell rang, cutting through his plotting. A growl rose in his throat. So help him, if that was Jason wanting more money, he might do anything at this point. He threw open the door already aggravated. When his gaze landed on the tiny brown-haired woman he called Mom and the burly asshole Mike, Nash's temper spiked.

"What?" He knew that was no way to greet his mom, but she had brought a snake to his home.

She didn't seem the least bit put off by his unwelcoming tone. Her amber-colored eyes held his stare. "You two need to put this feud behind you. I'm tired of stressing about it."

Nash's eyebrows rose at the claim. "There's no feud. I'm just fine to never speak again."

His mom shook her head. "Let's sit down and talk about it."

With a sigh, Nash took a step back and let them inside. It was his mom. He couldn't tell her to go away, but goddamn. He fucking hated Mike. The feeling was obviously mutual based on the look Mike shot him as he crossed the threshold. His green eyes flashed with malice. He matched Nash in height and muscle, but Nash wasn't worried. Nash rolled his eyes at the fury in Mike's stare and shut the door behind them. Mike wasn't paying Jason's rent. He didn't know what the guy had to be mad about.

While calling on his last drop of patience, Nash faced them. "Say what you came to say."

His mom jumped in first. "My birthday is coming up and I want all my boys together, but I know you won't show up with all this going on, so work it out."

No way would Nash get sucked into that guilt trip. He wasn't in the wrong. "I don't have to see everyone to see you. If you want, I'll take you to dinner or whatever. You'll always be my mom, but I'm done with this no-good fucker you married. You're the one determined to stay with someone who can't get his shit together or keep his hands to himself when he's high. That's on you. I've done all I can to help."

Mike let out a deep growl. "Look, boy. Jason always gets paid. His check might be late sometimes, but he always gets what he's owed. Leave your mom out of things."

Nash's temper snapped. "Jason might be your son, but he's still an employee. You know damn well you should be paying him on time, every time, but you never do, because you know you can get away with it. It's bullshit. Anyone else would have quit on your ass a long time ago, but he loves you. Only a complete bastard would keep taking advantage of that. I'm sick of paying his rent because you can't be bothered to pay his check. Is it not bad enough that he's likely to end up in prison for you someday?"

"He always gets paid," Mike said between clenched teeth. "If you choose to pay his rent and he doesn't pay you back, that's between you two. I don't know why you care anyways. You never cared what's happened to him in the past."

Nash wanted to put his fist through Mike's face. He couldn't believe the guy refused to acknowledge his part. He was an evil narcissist to his core. "I'm not saying Jason is innocent. Believe me, I've had words with him too. But all this bullshit starts with you, because I wouldn't have to cover his rent in the first damn place if you did your job. I've worked in that shop. I know you can pay him if you want. God knows you're fencing enough shit to pay fifty employees. This whole thing is like some fucked-up power trip to you. You live for seeing how far you can push people and I'm done with it." He focused on his mom. "Don't bring him here again. That's your husband. He's nothing to me. If you want—"

The doorbell rang, cutting him off. Nash eyed the door. Apparently, it was the day for unexpected visitors. He stormed the door, expecting it would be Jason. No doubt his mom had called him into this bullshit too. He yanked the door opened ready to blast Jason too if he wanted to join in. The moment his gaze landed on River; Nash damn near leapt from the house in his rush to close the door behind him so Mike wouldn't see him.

River's eyebrows rose. He was understandably shocked at Nash's reaction to seeing him. His features shifted, as if he realized his thoughts were showing. A bright smile stretched his lips. "Sorry to show up like this. I found your wallet on my couch. I considered waiting until tomorrow and taking it by your work on my lunch break, but I thought you might need it before then. It would ruin my weekend if my wallet went missing, and I didn't have your number." He snapped his teeth together—like he realized he was rambling.

Nash took the wallet from River and shoved it in his back pocket. He glanced over his shoulder making sure no one had opened the door when he wasn't looking. "Thanks. I appreciate it. I hadn't noticed it was missing."

River cast a look around, checking out the place. "This is nice. You acted like you live in a shanty while checking out my place yesterday."

He knew what River saw. A small brick home that was only big enough for two bedrooms. A tiny garage that was too small for Nash's Dodge Ram, his bike, and his tools. A quiet neighbor-hood with mostly elderly people or really young families. What River didn't see was the extra motorcycle behind his car. It was custom made with more stolen pieces than legal ones. River didn't know about the two people inside who had raised him to be someone River wouldn't be proud to know. He had to get River out of here.

Nash's brain itched with impatience. Mike couldn't see River. The guy already tormented Nash, trying to pull him back into his terrible circle of Hell. If he found out Nash was dating anyone, it was over. From trial and error, Mike knew he couldn't control Nash through Jason, but River was different. Nash wouldn't let him get hurt to save himself. Plus, Mike would probably say something awful to River and then Nash would have to kill him. His mom would never forgive that. "You have to go."

River's smile slipped away. He blinked. "Okay."

"Sorry. I'm in the middle of something."

River's gaze slid toward the door before meeting Nash's stare again. His expression said it all.

Nash had fucked any chance of being with River. "Okay. Like I said, I was just returning your wallet." He didn't wait for Nash to explain or try to fix things even a little. River turned away and jogged down the steps. Nash watched him go with his heart in his throat. River was the first sliver of happiness Nash had felt in a long time. This was all on Mike. With that nugget of anger fueling him, Nash ground his teeth until River backed out of the driveway and was gone. Then he threw the door open, prepared for battle. Mike would get the hell out of his house and his life. Then maybe Nash could find a way to apologize to River. He was done with all things family related. They always killed everything good.

He waved toward the door. "Time to go."

His mom wasn't having it. "I'm not going anywhere until this is settled."

Nash held her stare, ensuring she knew he was one hundred percent serious. "Mom, I love you, but I'm done with this. Take your husband and go while I'm still willing to talk to you."

With a nod, his mom stood and moved for the door. He could tell she had her teeth clenched. Nash hated that he hurt her, but he had to cut this poison from his life. Family was killing him, and he felt positive it wasn't supposed to be like that. They had probably already cost him River. The price of loyalty had gotten too high too many years ago to count. Today, they had surpassed his price range.

Chapter Four

SINCE WALKING AWAY FROM Nash the day before, River had tried several times to talk himself down from the ledge in his mind. He was being ridiculous. He felt stupid as hell for hurting this much. They had literally known each other a day. So they wouldn't be friends. Fine. Nash had saved him a hundred bucks by teaching him how to change his filter by himself. River had repaid him with dinner. End of story. Except for that kiss. That goddamn kiss had River swinging wildly between angrily cutting clients' hair to pressing his hand to his stomach, hoping to squelch the pain. His throat kept unexpectedly swelling. Several times, he had blinked away sneaky tears. River felt like an idiot. Maybe that was what it boiled down to. He had thought Nash liked him. He was such a goddamn fool. River damn near broke his favorite brush while cleaning it in his rage. Only someone stupid as hell would believe someone like Nash would ever want someone like him. He wasn't beautiful. Eyes didn't follow him. River didn't even have a sparkling personality. No one wanted him.

"Hey, River. You have a walk-in requesting you. Do you have time to squeeze them in before you go to lunch?"

He needed the distraction. River worked up a fake smile for the girl who worked the front counter. "Sure. Send them back."

River busied himself by grabbing a fresh cape. When he felt movement behind him, River turned and readied himself to fake his way through another cut. His smile slipped away at the sight of Nash. “No.”

Nash’s eyebrows rose. “No, what?”

“Get your hair cut somewhere else. I’m going to lunch.”

Nash shifted from foot to foot, looking sexy and awkward. Goddamn him. “Then let me take you to lunch.”

“No.”

“Then you can cut my hair. Either way, we’re talking, so you might as well have the scissors and the upper hand.”

That was true. A hint of evil rose inside him. It must have shown on his face because Nash looked worried. River patted the back of the seat. "Sit down."

With a shrug, Nash did as told. "As long as you hear me out, do your worst."

A wicked chuckle rose in River's throat. He swallowed it down. "I'm an artist first. I don't do bad work."

"That doesn't surprise me. I doubt you're bad at anything."

With an eye roll, River snapped the cape around Nash's neck a little tighter than necessary before spraying his hair in a way that probably drowned him. "Why are you here?"

"I need a haircut and I want to apologize for yesterday," Nash said with water dripping from his lips.

River brushed his hair rougher than necessary. "I don't want to hear it. What do you want me to do with your hair?"

"Whatever you want," Nash said, as if annoyed by the topic change. "Whether you want to hear it or not, I need to say it. I'm sorry."

"Good. You said it. Don't talk anymore." River angrily snatched up his electric razor and went to work. Nash's apology meant River wasn't imagining things. Nash hadn't wanted someone to see him yesterday. River moved closer to Nash's head as something peeked out at him beneath Nash's hair. His head was tattooed. River tried not to let that fact distract him. "Are you married?"

Nash snorted. “No.”

With his attention split between shaping Nash’s hair and his anger, River kept up the questioning. “Then I take it you live with someone.”

“Nope. I live alone. Before you ask, no. I’m not dating anyone either. It’s not at all what you think.”

River doubted Nash had any real clue what he thought. While Nash being a cheat had been one of his first thoughts, River believed something even worse. Nash didn’t want his friends to think he had any interest in someone like River. They didn’t match. Nash was muscles and tattoos. Motorcycles and bad boys. River was small and nothing. He was boring and plain. Damn. The unexpected tears were back. He would accept Nash’s apology, cut his hair, and let him go. That was the right thing to do. It was too bad River wouldn't get to look back on that kiss without the taint of Nash's shame. But truthfully, it never should have happened. They didn't match. He had to accept it.

River's silence was deafening. Hurt rolled off him in waves. It was obvious Nash hadn't fixed anything. He wished River would speak his piece so Nash could fix whatever was in his head. He had been so angry with himself after what happened, he had called in sick to work to talk to River. He had gone by River's house first, but he wasn't home. While Nash hadn't wanted to do this at River's job, he had to talk to him. He didn't give a fuck about his hair. This was him doing whatever it took to fix things. He liked River and Nash hadn't liked anyone in a long time. It was like Nash wasn't built for this day and age. He only met aggressive men. Nash didn't meet people like River. Sweet and guileless. River was adorable and endearing. It was sexier than River could possibly imagine. He fucked with Nash.

Nash was a protector by nature. He took care of people. While River didn't seem to need him, he still made Nash want to keep him safe. River made Nash want to build him a house and make sure his tires had enough air. He wanted to be River's man.

A brown-haired lady in a white lab coat walked by and then reversed course when her gaze landed on Nash. A smile lit her face. Her big blue eyes were the mirror image of River's.

She stepped forward with her hand extended. "Hi. I'm Dr. Charlotte Yearly. I don't think I've seen you around before. Welcome to Serenity Concepts."

Nash shook her hand. "Nash. It's nice to meet you."

She motioned in River's direction. "You're in great hands." Her gaze shifted River's way. "When you're done here, would you like to go to lunch?"

"I'd love to," River said, sounding absent. "I'm almost done. Nash just needs a bit of a beard trim and then he'll be finished."

"Are you River's mom?" Nash asked, jumping in and refusing to let this chance pass.

Blue eyes shifted back his way. "Yes. Sorry. I didn't mean to interrupt your appointment time."

Nash waved off her apology. “It’s no problem. I’m happy I’m getting the chance to meet you. River never brings me around.”

Her gaze sharpened and Nash swore he felt River’s stare biting into the back of his head. “Oh. You’re a friend of River’s. That’s great. I’ll admit I was a little concerned with what he’s attempting with your hair.”

Nash held on to his smile. “I told him he was free to do whatever he wanted.”

“That’s good, because he is,” Charlotte said with a laugh.

River snorted. “I’m giving him the look he deserves.”

Damn. Judging by River’s tone, he might be wearing a hat for the next six months. “It’s fine,”

Nash said, keeping his smile in place. "I trust him."

Charlotte's expression turned calculating. "Would you like to join us for lunch? River never introduces me to any of his friends."

River jumped in. "I'm sure Nash doesn't—"

"I'd love to," Nash said, speaking over River. "I've been looking forward to meeting you."

Charlotte beamed, obviously drawing her own conclusions. "I can't wait—like I said, River never brings anyone around."

"That's because there's no one to bring around," River said between clenched teeth as he trimmed Nash's beard.

Nash and Charlotte both ignored him. Nash held her stare, ensuring there would be no misunderstandings. "I'd be disappointed if he did, since he's already taken."

River released a tired-sounding sigh. Nash's smile grew. If River wanted to be rid of him, he would have to dump Nash properly now. Nash wasn't playing with River.

Charlotte's eyes flashed with humor. "I see I'm going to like you."

"The feeling is mutual." Nash was pretty sure River was one irritation away from stabbing Nash in the throat with his scissors. River used his neck duster to wipe away the stray beard hairs he had just trimmed. Their gazes collided. Nash couldn't hold back the heat that grew inside him as they stared at each other. River nervously looked away. An evil smile pulled at Nash's lips. River wasn't escaping him.

Once River noticed Nash's head was tattooed beneath his hair, he hadn't been able to stop himself from shaping Nash's hair in a way that showed off the dragon design. Mad or not, he was a stylist at heart. He couldn't fucking believe Nash had used his mom against him. Damned if River wasn't split right down the middle over the whole goddamn thing. While he was still angry over the way Nash had dismissed him, he equally wanted to happy dance over the way Nash had declared River as his with River's mom. He was such an irresistible combination of bad boy and responsible sexy man that River didn't know how to resist Nash.

He brushed the hair from Nash's neck. "Let's go wash your hair. If we're going to lunch, I don't want you sitting there with a bunch of loose hairs everywhere."

His mom nodded. "Go do that. I'll hang up my coat and lock up while you finish."

Nash dutifully stood and followed River to the wash station. River did his best not to meet Nash's stare as he settled in and River wet what was left of his hair. Nash obviously had decided he wouldn't stand for being ignored.

"I like you, River. A lot."

River refused to be budged, but he listened. He was open to hearing Nash's apology.

"I'm so sorry about yesterday. My stepdad was there, and we were arguing. I knew if he saw you that he would drag you into everything because he's a complete ass who hates me."

That brought River's gaze to Nash's. "So you were hiding me. Are you ashamed?"

"Yes and no." River wanted to appreciate his honesty, but he didn't hide. Nash didn't leave things there. "I'm not ashamed, but I was hiding you from him. Trust me, you don't want to get in his sights. He's a terrible person. It wouldn't matter to him that you're a stranger or a good person. He would go after you in a heartbeat if he thought it would hurt me."

River went back to watching his hands. He didn't want Nash to see his heart. "Would it hurt you?"

"Yes."

Against all good sense, River thawed a bit. "I guess we'll see at lunch if you're ashamed."

"I guess we will," Nash said, sounding confident.

River focused on towel drying Nash's hair. He dug his comb from his stylist coat and swept Nash's hair to one side. Against his will, a smile tugged at River's lips. Nash was so fucking sexy. He looked like a Viking with those head tattoos showing. River's smile fell. He had never wanted to be with anyone else like he did Nash. Life was cruel like that.

"It breaks my heart watching your smile disappear." River's gaze snapped to Nash's at the claim. Nash looked sincere. River couldn't look away. "You're beautiful. I want to make you smile again."

Goddamn. He looked like he was being real. River was scared to hope. He unsnapped Nash's cape and tossed it aside. "Go check out your hair and tell me what you think."

With a nod, Nash stood and moved to the closest mirror. He turned his head from side to side, inspecting River's work. "You did good. The way your mom talked, I expected to find you had shaved me bald."

A chuckle escaped River without warning. "Truthfully, she was probably a tiny bit horrified by the tattoos. But now I know she would accept even Satan, as long as she thinks there's any hope I have a boyfriend."

Nash turned his way. He kept River frozen in place with his heated stare as he closed the distance between them. "I promise I'm not Satan, but you do have a boyfriend now."

Against his will, River blushed and turned shy. "Do I?"

Nash nodded. “You do.” He moved slow, lowering his head. River refused to meet him halfway. Nash lightly kissed the corner of River’s mouth. River’s breathing immediately deepened. There was nothing sexual about the kiss. Nash didn’t touch him in any other way, but River’s heart still tried beating from his chest. He couldn’t stay angry.

“Are you boys ready?”

Nash straightened away and flashed River’s mom a smile. “Yes.”

River slipped off his coat. It took every bit of his willpower not to look his mom’s way while he dropped the jacket at his station. Nash patiently waited. The moment River was within arm’s length, Nash took his hand. They walked to the back door together. River fought an out-of-control smile. He felt so giddy. It was ridiculous. Nash claimed to be his boyfriend. Wow. This sexy guy was really holding his hand. His cheeks kept heating. He felt like a teenager.

"We'll take my car," Charlotte said over her shoulder.

Nash nodded. His gaze shot River's way, as if he remembered something last second. "Oh, I didn't pay. How much do I owe you?"

Before River could answer, his mom did. "Don't worry about that. We don't charge family."

River nearly groaned. His mom was definitely that mom. She wanted him married, settled, and adopting her some grand babies. At this rate, she would scare Nash off before they even got started.

River glanced Nash's way, catching his attention. "Sorry," he mouthed, hoping to blunt any damage his mom's over-enthusiasm caused today.

Nash winked. His smile said he wasn't bothered. River hoped that was true. If he knew his mom, she was about to test him.

On the way to the restaurant, Nash sat in the backseat and stared at River's profile. So far, things were looking up, but he wouldn't feel confident until they were alone. That tiny slice of time he had gotten with River at the salon gave him hope. River hadn't pulled away when Nash kissed him. Later, he would get the kiss he needed. Even to Nash, his stare felt hungry. River glanced over his shoulder, as if he felt it too. A blush tinted his cheeks before he looked away. Nash's hunger doubled.

Charlotte chose a place Nash had never been. He played the gentleman, opening her door before rushing to open River's. River almost beat him to it. Luckily, Nash got there just in time to help him from the car so he could keep a hold on River's hand on the way to the door. River didn't pull away. When they reached their table, Nash pulled out the chair for Charlotte before doing the same for River and claiming a seat at his side. He immediately reached for River beneath the table. His smile was out of control when River reached for him at the same time. He bit his bottom lip and stared at the menu, hoping to hide his happiness.

"So, Nash, what do you do for a living?"

Nash focused on Charlotte. "I'm a mechanic at the Nissan dealership. That's where I met River."

Charlotte's gaze swung River's way. "You didn't tell me you had a problem with your car."

"I didn't. It was recalled. It's fine now. Nash fixed it."

Her smile turned luminous. "That's great. Every family needs a mechanic."

River huffed. "Mom. Stop."

He sounded so horrified that Nash couldn't stop smiling. "I'm teaching River how to do some minor things himself so no one can take advantage of him."

The way Charlotte laughed piqued Nash's curiosity. "I can't imagine how that's going. One time, River's dad tried to teach him how to change his oil. Somehow, River managed to cut himself so badly, he needed stitches. Neither of us could explain how it happened, but Todd never tried again."

"There was a sharp spot under the hood," River said under his breath like he was pouting.

Nash's hunger tripled. Damn. He was snagged. Nash brought River's hand to his mouth and kissed it. River's gaze slid his way. A sweet smile touched his lips. Nash wanted him alone. He forced himself to focus on Charlotte.

"Sometimes, it's the sneakiest sharp pieces that get you. I've needed stitches a few times."

A waitress appeared before Charlotte could respond. Nash expected Charlotte would order first, but the woman was completely focused on Nash. "May I take your order?"

Nash cast a glance around the table.

Charlotte shrugged. “I’m ready, if you two are.”

The waitress’s gaze never wavered from Nash. He moved closer to River, ensuring she understood they were together before nodding River’s way. “I believe this one has a sweet tooth. He wants the chocolate overload cake and a root beer.”

River chuckled. His eyes danced with humor. He nodded. “I do.” He motioned Nash’s way. “And this one wants the gumbo and a beer. Something local.”

A laugh rose in Nash’s throat. That was a hell of a guess. “Yep.”

Charlotte passed her menu the waitress’s way, snagging the girl’s attention. “All three of us will be having the grilled chicken with salads and I’m paying.”

Nash fought a laugh at the obvious chastisement in Charlotte's tone. He lowered his voice for River's ears alone. "I'll buy you a chocolate cake later."

River leaned into his side, snuggling close. "I make a killer gumbo. That's what I'll fix for dinner tonight, if you're interested."

"Always." Nash held River's stare as he made the claim, hoping River realized it was more of a vow. They were a couple now. River would be seeing a lot of him.

Proving how much River's mom liked Nash, she had given River the rest of the day off after lunch. River had to admit Nash had been charming. He definitely had River ready to take off his pants. Staying true to his word, Nash had followed River home so River could drop off his car, and then he had bought River a chocolate cake. He had also paid for all of River's groceries. River had tried balking, but Nash reminded him of their deal. He would pay for the food so River could keep cooking him amazing meals. Nash made River sound like he was some gourmet chef. He bragged to the cashier that River would make him fat. By the end of the day, River's face hurt from smiling. He never expected this overwhelming happiness. With his hip leaned into the counter, River watched Nash load the dishwasher. He looked relaxed and content—like a well-fed cat. In Nash's case, a lion, but whatever. "Is it okay if I ask you a question?"

Nash shot him a quick look. "Of course."

"Why would you get such an intricate tattoo on your head and then grow your hair out where no one can see it?"

"I have a lot of tattoos," Nash said with a shrug, piquing River's interest. "Most of them I can hide with clothing. I like them, but people look at you different when you have a lot of ink. You'd think they wouldn't these days, but they do. I get treated like a criminal, so I keep it hidden."

"Oh no, and then I uncovered it. I'm sorry."

Nash turned the water off and moved to box River in against the counter. He stared down at River with his heart in his eyes. "Don't do that. I like what you did. You showed that you like me for me. That means a lot to me."

Heat climbed River's face. "I think it's sexy."

With a single step, the lower half of Nash's body collided with River. River's mouth went dry. Nash was hard all over and equally big everywhere. "I think you're sexy," Nash said, blanking River's mind.

River's hands found Nash's hips like a magnet. His nerves took ahold of his tongue. "I'd say you don't have to lie to me to get in my pants, but I wouldn't know, and I like it a little too much to complain."

Nash blinked at River's oversharing. "Wait." He looked shell-shocked. "Are you saying you're a virgin?"

River curled his nose at the question. "Virginity is an archaic belief meant to shame people through religion while allowing fathers to charge a higher price when selling their daughters into marriage."

"Oh my god." Nash sounded horrified. "You are a virgin. How is that possible? You're twenty-four."

The level of exposure River felt was nearly crippling. Nash was super-hot, and River already didn't match. Now he had to try to explain how he had never had sex. It was horrifying. River focused on Nash's chest. He couldn't meet the man's stare. "Um, well, I guess I've never really liked anyone that much and I'm not typically an overly sexual person. Although I feel like my sex drive has been set to hyper speed since meeting you, but that's a different story." The rambling wouldn't stop. The more River's discomfort grew, the faster he talked, and the more he confessed. "It's just that sex is very personal, and I don't belong in this hookup generation. I guess I thought I would run into someone at the grocery store one day and our gazes would meet, and I would be overcome." The heat in his face doubled. "Jesus, I don't know. I just never said yes, I guess. It never felt like the right time."

Nash touched River's chin and forced River's gaze to his. River's breath caught at Nash's expression. He looked hard and possessive. River was paralyzed. "You're perfect." River's heart melted at the claim. Then Nash's lips touched his. "A sexy treasure," Nash said, changing directions. River found himself clinging to Nash's hands where Nash cupped his face, scared he would pull away. He didn't want this sweet moment to end. The way their tongues stroked—almost reverently. Nash's kiss turned into an innocent brushing of lips. He felt Nash smile against his skin. "Let's go make out. I promise to let you keep your clothes."

River wouldn't make that same vow.

As River led Nash to his bedroom, Nash beat back the dark hunger rising inside him. He couldn't get past River's confession. Not the part about being a virgin. River was right about that. Virginity was a myth. There were too many forms of sex to say when innocence was lost. It was the admission that he thought he would run into someone at the grocery store someday. That was the exact thought Nash had when he met River. It was almost like he had been shown a sign. They were meant to meet. They were headed somewhere. This was real.

River's room looked nothing like what Nash would have pictured. Everything was black. Nash gave it a cursory glance before his eyes were back on River. When they had gotten settled in for the night, River had taken a quick shower and changed. The tiny shorts were back, except these were cotton pj shorts that clung to his skin. Nash's mouth watered as River crawled onto the bed. He didn't know if he could keep his promise. Nash really wanted those shorts on the floor.

He didn't stop moving until he settled between River's thighs and stared down at him. There was so much trust in River's huge blue eyes. Nash couldn't let him down. "How can you not know how sexy you are? That blows me away. I'm giving myself all sorts of internal lectures to keep from falling on you with my dick out."

A smile exploded across River's face. "That's only funny because I'm wishing you would."

His cock twitched at the claim. “You have no idea how you tempt me.”

River’s hands slipped beneath Nash’s t-shirt. He caressed Nash’s sides while dragging the material higher. “I want to see you.”

Nash had to take a breath at River’s words. He was turned on past the point of painful. Nash sat back on his heels and quickly peeled off his shirt.

River stroked his stomach. “Goddamn.”

At the curse, Nash’s gaze shot to River’s face. His cheeks were flushed, and he looked ready to get fucked. The temptation was crippling. He swept a glance down River’s body. His erection couldn’t be missed in the thin cotton shorts. Something inside Nash broke.

"I said I'd let you keep your clothes. I didn't say you wouldn't come in them." That was all the warning Nash gave before he claimed River's mouth. His hips rolled. Nash openly humped River, using the pressure and friction between them to drive River insane. The way River went wild beneath him was another chink in Nash's armored resolve. River's short fingernails dug into his back. He bit Nash's bottom lip as he moved restlessly beneath Nash. River grabbed the headboard and held on as his hips left the bed. He openly used Nash's body in his fight to find pleasure. Nash feared himself in the face of River's unabashed passion. The blushing innocent was gone. The man beneath him had needs that Nash could fulfill.

To his surprise, River released the headboard and pushed at Nash's chest. Nash obeyed his silent commands until River had Nash on his back and straddled his body. He kissed Nash hard and deep even as he tore at the front of Nash's jeans. Nash was helpless to stop him. His entire body hummed as his cock filled River's hand. His muscles seized. Nash damn near came from only the skin on skin contact. He couldn't do this. Nash was about to thoroughly disappoint River.

He rolled, pinning River beneath him. Without a qualm, he shoved at the front of River's shorts, setting his erection free. "Technically, you're still in your clothes," Nash said as he slithered down River's body. He didn't give River time to think before he swallowed River's cock. A loud moan caressed his ears. Nash didn't hold back. He licked and sucked before swallowing.

River strained against him. “Nash. Oh, damn. That’s so good. I want you.” The neediness in River’s cries had Nash ready to give in and fuck him. He swore he could already feel River’s tight heat. He chose a different path. After shooting upward and reclaiming River’s mouth, Nash shoved his jeans down his hips just enough to free him to make love to Nash. Their erections brushed. Nash thrust like he wanted to do inside River, rubbing their cocks together. River’s cries vibrated around Nash’s tongue. Nash was ready to blow. This was hands down the best sex he had ever had, and he hadn’t even gotten inside River. It was River. He was so goddamn responsive. He didn’t hide. River loved being pleasured, and he obviously didn’t care if Nash knew.

River's entire body stiffened. Nash swore the universe held its breath. An orgasm slammed into Nash as a cry ripped from River's throat. Hot cum filled the space between them as Nash scratched to hold on to his sanity. All he could do was open-mouthed fight for air. His entire body shook. This one belonged to him. River would never get away if Nash had anything to say about it. Crazy thoughts rattled around inside his head. Idea after idea of how he could keep River tied to his side flared to life. He kissed River deep and plotted. It was time to fully snip the ties with his family. They would destroy Nash with this truth. Nash wouldn't hide River. He couldn't risk losing this. Nash had never felt so whole.

Chapter Five

River was a complete wreck. Despite his mom's claims to Nash to the contrary, and even though it had been years, he had introduced her to a couple of men in the past. She had hated both of them. For good reason, of course. However, River had never introduced a man to his father. This was the ultimate test for Nash to pass. River hadn't told Nash that when he asked him to come to this family cookout. By the time River heard the growl of Nash's Harley coming down the drive, he was forcing himself to not bite his nails. If his dad didn't like Nash, River didn't think it would change anything, but he really wanted his dad to like Nash.

River couldn't tear his gaze away from his dad. He needed to see his very first reaction to seeing Nash. Otherwise, he might never know how his dad really felt.

"There he is," his mom said loudly, letting River know Nash had appeared.

His dad turned away from the grill. A bright smile lit his face. River couldn't get a read on him. "Well, come on back and join us. We don't bite. Not on the first date anyhow. We like to wait until at least the third meeting before getting a taste."

River covered his eyes.

"Stop," his mom fussed, pulling River's hand away from his face. "Your dad has never actually bitten anyone." An odd expression crossed her features. "At least, no men that I know of."

River shook his head. "Why do you two always have to be weirdos?"

Charlotte shrugged. "Everyone should be so lucky. Just think, you could have gotten normal parents. How boring."

River's gaze slid Nash's way. He forgot to respond, and he swore his heart sighed as he watched Nash shake hands with his dad. In dark jeans and a black V-neck t-shirt, Nash looked as sexy as always. His amber gaze slid River's way. A sweet smile touched Nash's lips. River bit back a sigh. He was gorgeous. Heart-stopping.

Nash's voice floated River's way. "It's nice to meet you, Mr. Yearly."

"It's Todd," his dad said, motioning toward the table and inviting Nash to sit. "Charlotte has been telling me all about you. I'm glad you could make it tonight."

Nash claimed the lawn chair at River's side. He kissed the corner of River's mouth before focusing on River's dad again. "Thanks for the invitation. River is always telling me stories about both of you. I feel like I know you already, but I'm glad to finally get to spend some time with you."

His dad looked thrilled that Nash actually wanted to be there. Nash looked relaxed and not the least bit nervous. River tried breathing a quiet sigh of relief. He wouldn't know his dad's real thoughts on Nash until his mom gave him the scoop later, but things seemed okay for now.

River listened to them talk with half an ear as he focused on the way Nash's thumb stroked River's hand beneath the table. Nash held hands with him so confidently, as if it would always be this way. A lump formed in River's throat. No one knew how badly he wanted this life. A solid and steady love at his side.

"I hope you're hungry. Todd made his famous spicy steaks. He's an awesome cook."

Before Nash could respond, Todd released a loud "Oooh." His smile said River should hide. River froze in anticipation of whatever embarrassing horror was sure to come. His dad didn't let him down. "Charlotte, do you remember how River couldn't say 'hungry' when he was little?"

"No." River's choked horror didn't slow his parents.

"Oh my god," Charlotte said, laughing. She focused on Nash, and River knew he couldn't stop it from happening. "So, River couldn't pronounce 'hungry.' It always came out sounding like 'horny.' Of course, he didn't know what that word meant or why we would always try to cover his mouth anytime we went out to eat or to visit family. I swear it was his life's mission to tell everyone he was horny. Every time we were at a restaurant, he would scream, 'I'm horny, Momma. I'm horny.' I swear we almost stopped going out." His mom laughed loudly.

A sexy chuckle rumbled from Nash.

River leaned forward and set his forehead on the table. It would be a long night. He had always been awkward and stupid. His parents had countless ammunition to use against him. Only the sensation of Nash's palm running up his inner thigh saved River from leaving right then. All he could do was hope his parents got their embarrassing stories out of the way tonight so they could have peaceful dinners in the future. River didn't know who he was kidding. His parents loved to keep him humble.

Charlotte and Todd lived in a gated community in a huge house with a garden and a pool. The place was nothing like where Nash had been raised on the edge of the ghetto. River's parents were the opposite of Nash's in every way. He adored them. With every story River's parents shared, Nash felt himself digging an inch deeper into River's life. He wanted that. He wanted this. Even though River spent the whole night blushing and hiding his face, Nash wanted more. He wanted all the memories of River's childhood. His phone buzzed several times during the night. He ignored it, not wanting to be rude. The first moment everyone else was otherwise occupied, Nash checked it.

Mom: *Mike doesn't have any help tonight. Jason is out of town.*

Mom: *You know I wouldn't ask, but I'm worried Mike will get hurt if he tries pulling a job alone.*

Mom: *I understand why you're not answering my texts. I know I shouldn't ask, but there really isn't anyone else.*

Mom: *The money will be good and I promise it would only be one time.*

A hollow pit opened in Nash's gut. There was a child inside him, wishing his mom was a good person. He wished she loved him like a normal mom. Nash wished her love didn't hinge so much on what Nash could do for her. He hadn't heard from her since she came to his house to talk about Jason. It had been all about Mike then too. Nash knew she hadn't really cared if he came around for her birthday. She had never loved anyone as much as she did the man who beat her kids and kept her down. But Nash's whole life, he hadn't given up hope that she would care about him.

Nash's gaze slid River's way. He stood between his parents, giving the pair hugs and saying his goodbyes. River had no idea how much his parents loved him. While they went out of their way to embarrass him, it was all done in love. They knew how to weed out the weak. They wanted a good and strong man for their son. Nash hadn't always been good, but he wasn't going anywhere. As he looked on, River's mom toyed with River's hair and asked about his finances. She wanted to know how much food was in his fridge and if he had gas in his car. Nash's chest hurt. His eyes burned. He glanced back down at his phone and read through his messages once more. Then he blocked his mom's number.

River's dad jogged down the front steps, heading Nash's way. Nash stuffed his phone in his back pocket and smiled. River looked like his dad. While his eyes were exactly like his mom's, River had gotten everything else from his father. Todd was short and dark-haired like River, except there was some gray mixed in and his eyes crinkled in the corners from where he obviously smiled a lot. Now was no different.

"Thanks again for coming tonight," Todd said, shaking Nash's hand. "I know we can be a bit much, but River is the only child we were blessed with, and—"

"It's fine," Nash said, cutting him off. "I had a great time. River might be a little traumatized, but I had fun." They exchanged a few more words while Nash's true focus was on River. Todd rejoined Charlotte on the porch, and they headed inside as River moved his way. Their gazes locked and held. River bit his lip, as if fighting a smile. He looked at Nash like he cared—like he wanted Nash for Nash. Like no one else ever had. Nash's stomach growled as River came to stand toe to toe with him.

River lost the battle against his smile. "Are you still hungry? Those steaks were extra spicy tonight. I think Dad was testing your mettle."

"Yeah. I'm still horny."

River punched him in the arm even as a blush exploded through his cheeks. "Ugh. Don't make fun of me. I was like four."

Nash's cheeks ached as he rubbed the place where River's blow landed, even though it didn't hurt. "What? I said what I meant."

River's expression shifted, turning playful. "In that case, we should go back to my place, don't you think? I have exactly what you need."

Nash forgot all things parent-related as he stared at the man he wanted more than oxygen. "I like this plan." He tucked a loose strand of hair behind River's ear. "I'll follow you home."

"Okay." River shuffled closer. Nash's heart beat a little faster. River's hands slid up Nash's chest as he went up onto his toes. Nash met him halfway. Their lips barely brushed in the most innocent of kisses, and Nash's heart was as snagged as ever. River was his drug. Nash couldn't enough. He planned to invade every corner of River's life, ensuring he couldn't get away. As their lips brushed again, Nash acknowledged he might be a little too obsessed, but River belonged to him. Nash would get the life he had never had but always craved. River's every touch promised him as much.

Chapter Six

NASH: *I GOT A job offer a while back to work for a shop close to your work. Out of loyalty to the dealership, I didn't take it, even though it's more money. They sent me another offer today. It's even more money. I'm considering it. What do you think?*

River: *What would make you the happiest?*

Nash: *I'm already happy, but this is more money, no weekends, and closer to you. Plus, it comes with one hell of a sign-on bonus that I'd love to spend on you.*

River: *I'm already spoiled. You don't need to spend money on me. As to the job, it sounds a little like you already have your mind made up about it. I have to admit, I love the thought of having you to myself on the weekends. What are the cons?*

Nash: *I'd be losing some vacation time, and I'd have to change insurances.*

River: *Maybe tell them you'll think about it and we can toss around all the pros and cons tonight when I get to your place. You can use me as a sounding board.*

Nash: *Wear the tiny shorts.*

River: *Will you still want to discuss work if I'm barely dressed?*

Nash: *I promise we'll still figure out my next move, but I'm also planning to seduce you. So, you know, pencil me in for that.*

River: *lol. I miss you.*

Nash: *I miss you too. Hurry home.*

As River drove to Nash's place, he fought the urge to blush and chew off his bottom lip. Since they had officially started dating, they had spent every night together, but Nash hadn't pushed for sex. River was ready. In fact, he always had a hard time keeping his hands to himself now that he had seen Nash's nude body. Goddamn. He was amazing. Just solid and cuddly. So sexy. River's nonexistent sex drive was a thing of the past. There was something about Nash. It was like he had touched River's heart and somehow flipped the switch to his cock. River's mom said that probably meant he was demisexual. He should probably stop telling her everything, but really, it was too late to stop their friendship now and River had to tell someone. He had it bad.

By the time River made it to Nash's house, he practically danced his way to the door in his excitement to see Nash. They no longer knocked at each other's houses. He let himself in. The moment he stepped inside and his gaze landed on where Nash sat on the couch, his heart practically sighed.

Nash's eyes flashed with hunger as they landed on River. "Hey, baby. Strip."

Shock had River slow to react. "What?"

Nash flipped up the hem of his shirt, revealing his condom-covered erection. “Get in here and strip.”

A smile stretched River’s lips. “Have you been sitting here stroking yourself while waiting for me?”

Nash motioned toward a bottle of lube River hadn’t noticed. “Yes. I’m impatient.”

River kicked the door closed behind him. “Thank god.” River was out of his clothes so fast, it was Nash’s turn to look shocked.

“Wow. That has to be some kind of record.”

River climbed into Nash’s lap. “What can I say? I want you inside me. I’ve been prepping for you for what feels like forever, but you never seem interested. I’m interested.”

A sexy rumble of deep laughter slipped from Nash's lips as he palmed River's bare ass. "Oh, I'm interested. I've been trying to wait until you're ready. The last thing I want is for you to think this is all I want."

River chuckled as he tried kissing Nash's neck. "I don't think that."

"Glad we established that," Nash said, coming to his feet and leaving River no other choice but to cling to his body like a monkey. River shook with laughter as Nash scooped up the lube, held tightly to River, and raced for the bedroom.

At the edge of the bed, their lips clung as River fought to get Nash out of his clothes without giving up his kiss. The moment he finally had Nash nude, the air changed. Nash crowded River's space until his body covered River's on the bed. Their kiss turned sweet even as it deepened. River's body felt like it heated by ten degrees. Nash's hand skimmed down River's body, making goosebumps rise in its wake. He urged River's knee higher. Lube-coated fingers probed at River's asshole—like Nash was a multi-tasking magician. He fingered and stretched while taking short breaks to massage that internal spot that had River a panting hot mess. His heart made all sorts of noises. He felt too much. Nash's fingers disappeared. Something much larger pressed against River's hole. His body automatically tensed. That was the wrong move. It hurt more than he liked as Nash tried pushing inside. Nash immediately retreated when River sucked in a sharp breath.

"Change of plans," Nash said, rolling onto his back. "You get to be on top."

For half a second, River thought Nash was giving up on him until his words penetrated River's lust. He scrambled to straddle Nash's body. With his weight balanced on his knees and sitting back on his ankles, River's gaze ate up the sight of Nash between his thighs. A drop of pre-cum rolled down his length. He was so turned on, he could barely breathe. Nash stared up at him, looking equally desperate.

Nash stroked River's cock while River watched. As he looked on, Nash swiped his thumb across River's crown, stealing his pre-cum before bringing his thumb to his lips and licking away the moisture. River almost came right then. He was unaccustomed to Nash's blatant carnal nature. Nash even looked wicked—like he reveled in River's flavor. River's entire body practically vibrated with arousal. Nash stroked

River's erection again. A loud pant slipped past River's lips. Nash urged River to lift his weight. His cock probed at River's asshole again while he played with River's dick. All River could do was hang on and try to breathe. This time, River was too distracted to tense as Nash pushed inside. He was torn between feeling too full and wanting to ride Nash's palm. Then Nash changed angles. River saw stars. He already knew he would never touch himself again without remembering this moment. Nothing mattered but reaching orgasm. He felt half crazed.

With his head thrown back and sucking air, River openly rode Nash's cock and palm, straining toward the edge of madness.

"River. Holy shit. Damn, baby. You look so goddamn sexy on my dick. Fuck. Don't stop."

The words barely reached him. River was too far gone. Pressure climbed his cock. River held his breath. His every muscle tightened. The world exploded. Wave after wave of pleasure rocked him to his core. He might have melted, incapable of doing anything more than gasping through the ecstasy, but Nash rolled, pinning River beneath him. He thrust, pounding inside River at the perfect angle to completely wreck River's mind. Nash cried out while River clung to him, grasping at the wisps of his sanity. Nash was stuck with him now. River was an addict. He needed this forever. Goddamn. River was in love.

A thousand times, Nash told himself to be still. Stop petting River. He couldn't. His hands kept moving, stroking every place he could reach. His lips kept latching on to River's skin like a magnet. In his life, Nash had been with more people than he cared to admit. No one had rocked him to his soul the way River had. Nothing about River was an act. He owned everything he felt and showed it to Nash without shame. No one understood what being with River was like to Nash. His whole life, he had been surrounded by thieves and liars. People with secrets. River was pure and good. He was beautiful and honest. His heart was sexy as fuck. Nash didn't want to do anything other than what he did right then. Holding River was like holding heaven.

Without an ounce of shame, Nash could admit he was ass over tea kettle in love with River. Only the fact that River didn't know his past kept him from saying the words. One day, they would have to have that talk. When it happened, if River left, Nash thought he might survive it if River didn't know how sickeningly in love he was. Was it a ridiculous belief system? Yes, but Nash never claimed to possess an ounce of sanity.

"I'm taking the job offer."

River peeked one eye open at Nash's words. "When I left work, I realized there's a mechanic shop three doors down from us."

Nash smiled. He wasn't surprised River worked at the same place his whole life and just now noticed what was right down the street. He was oddly blind to a lot of obvious things. "That's the place."

"Yay," River cheered softly. "I can visit you on my lunch breaks and vice versa, if you want."

"I want."

River's smile turned bashful. "So," he said, dragging out the word. "You're taking a job within a stone's throw of me. Well, I couldn't throw a rock that far, but most people could."

A chuckle caught in Nash's throat. "You'll be stuck with me soon."

River rolled over, facing Nash. He tossed a leg over Nash and scooted closer. "That's cool. You're already stuck with me, so that's fair."

Nash couldn't help but touch him. He palmed River's hip. "You say that now, but I haven't started showing up every day, bugging you at work, and drooling down your neck."

“Drooling?”

Nash nodded. “Staring at your ass does that to me.”

An adorable snort caressed Nash’s ears. “If I see you outside, I’ll poke my head out the door and catcall you. You can sue my mom for employing a pervert.” River played with Nash’s beard, threatening to put him to sleep.

His eyes fell closed as he savored River’s touch. “I don’t think I’ve ever been catcalled.”

“I’d be honored to be your first.” The heavy laughter in River’s voice had Nash trying to move even closer.

“Speaking of first times, how are you feeling?”

River blushed. Pride and possessiveness filled Nash. “I’m good.”

"You're beautiful."

The embarrassment left River's features. His gaze sharpened, as if he hung on Nash's words. "You make me feel that way."

Something about that response bugged Nash, but he couldn't put his finger on it. Sometimes, he just got a feeling—like River believed he was ugly or something. It was weird. River never said anything blatantly insulting about himself. Nash couldn't explain it. He refused to stop telling River all the words. "I've never been this happy. It's kind of terrifying, knowing how easily you could crush me for such a tiny thing."

"You say the bravest things. It makes me really proud, thinking you want me."

There it was again. Just something odd Nash couldn't explain. "Does this not feel like knowing it?" Nash asked while running his hand up River's thigh.

A flush immediately rose on River's cheeks, making his eyes seem even bluer than normal. "You should kiss me."

Nash didn't hesitate to press his lips to River's. He felt a tiny hitch in River's breathing. Nash's heart needed more. "Let's stay right here all night. I'll order some pizza and we can eat right here and just steal all the minutes together."

"I love this idea," River said, coming back for more kisses.

As their tongues met and stroked, Nash wished he never had to work again. He had never been this enamored by anyone. Being with River made him not want to do anything else. Nash had already turned his notice in at work so he could be a few miles closer during the day. River felt more like an obsession than someone he dated. Nash wanted to be crazy and stare at River while he slept every night. He constantly fought the urge to show up unannounced at his work and beg for scraps of his time. More than once, he had taken the long way back from his lunch break to drive past his work. If River found out about his past and was done, Nash feared himself a little. He wasn't okay without River any longer.

Chapter Seven

RIVER: *DO YOU CARE if I come hang out with you on my lunch break?*

Nash: *I'll come to you.*

River: *Okay. Do you not want your work buddies to see me? Lol*

Nash: *I don't want you walking in this heat. It's a hundred and two outside.*

River: *Okay. I'll see you in a few.*

Nash: *Do we need anything from the store?*

River: *So much stuff. It might be easier if we go together.*

Nash: *I don't mind. Hit me with a list. I've got this. I can follow orders.*

River: *That sounds fun. I might have to try it one night.*

Nash: *or every night.*

River: *Promises. Promises.*

Five minutes until lunch, River remembered his forgotten lunch sack. He swallowed a huff. It wouldn't be a big deal, but he had left it at Nash's place, and he had ridden to work with Nash. Since he had been spending almost every night with Nash or vice versa, and they worked right down the street from each other now, they had started carpooling. It made sense since they worked similar hours and were headed in the same direction. In fact, River loved the arrangement. He didn't love going hungry, though.

He lightly brushed the hair from Veronica's shoulders, trying to decide what to do. He could walk down to Nash's work, but River wasn't certain what time he went to lunch. Maybe his mom would grab him something while she was out. He hadn't eaten breakfast, and he was notoriously bitchy when he didn't eat all day.

"Hey, gorgeous. I brought you lunch."

River's gaze shot to the doorway where Nash hovered with a bag and two drinks.

At the moment, River was hard pressed to decide which he was happier to see: the man or the food. Both were equally necessary to River's existence. A bright smile snapped to River's lips. "Hey. You're an absolute lifesaver. I just realized I forgot my lunch."

Nash's eyes twinkled with devilry. "I know. I saw it on the counter before we left, and I intentionally didn't grab it so I'd have an excuse to stop by."

As if he needed a reason. River wanted Nash around always.

"Is this the boyfriend?" Veronica asked before River could say as much. It couldn't have been more obvious River had been bragging about him.

"I know," Nash said loudly before River could respond. He was smiling like an idiot. "It's not fair, is it? River is surrounded by beautiful women like you all day, and I'm the fool who won him. It's not right, but I'm not looking a gift horse in the mouth. I know I won the lottery."

River shook his head. Nash was ridiculous. River was stupid in love with him.

The way Veronica laughed said Nash's ridiculousness worked. "I like this one, River."

River fought hard not to dance in place with happiness. He handed Veronica a mirror and turned her chair so she could check out the back of her hair. "I like him too. What do you think?"

She barely glanced in the mirror. "Amazing, as always. What do you two have planned for lunch?"

"Who are you, Mr. Studly? And can I get your number?" Geoff said, appearing from nowhere. He circled Nash like a vulture. "Delicious." Geoff was their most requested massage therapist. River tried stamping down the jealousy that immediately stirred in his gut. Geoff was blond and beautiful. Everyone loved his naughtiness and men swarmed to him like flies. River couldn't compete. Normally, Geoff was in the back with a client or gone for the day when Nash stopped by. River had been lucky to keep Nash away from him this long.

Annoyance flashed in Nash's eyes. He didn't look Geoff's way as he motioned toward River. "I'm with him."

Without thought, River pressed his lips together, fighting his smile.

"You can come see me next," Geoff said, practically purring the words. "I'm a big boy. I know how to wait my turn."

Nash focused on Geoff. His voice hardened. "I'm with him."

To River's surprise, Geoff stepped around Nash and walked away. It was so completely out of character for Geoff to give up on prey so easily that River found himself blinking in surprise as he watched him head out. Before he could say anything and give away how happy Nash had made him with that shutdown, his mom poked her head around the corner.

"Hey, Roni. We still on for lunch?"

Veronica nodded and pushed from the chair. "You bet, lady. Just let me pay and we can go."

His mom's gaze slid Nash's way. A smile lit her face. "Oh, hey. I see you got to meet my future son-in-law."

A hot blush flooded River's cheeks. "Mom." Even River heard the horror in his voice.

She rearranged her features, trying to look innocent. "What? I can hope and he got you into bed, which is more than anyone else can say."

River turned his chin up and stared at the ceiling. He couldn't believe this was happening. "Well, I can die now."

A sexy rumble of laughter was the only sound that penetrated his horror. Strong arms encircled his waist. A hard body pressed against back.

"I'm locking up behind me. You two have the place for an hour."

River finally managed to drop his chin at his mom's called words. She was gone. Warm lips brushed his nape.

"A whole hour alone. What should we do?"

"You could kill me, so I don't have to live through the humiliation of my mother for another day."

"I think she's cute," Nash said against the side of River's neck. "You're lucky. Not everyone has a mom they can confide in." Nash's hands slid down River's body. "Goddamn," Nash breathed. "It's crazy how much I've missed you this morning."

The embarrassment fled. Nothing existed but the man holding him. River sank into Nash's hold. “Same. You make me wish I didn’t have to do anything else.”

Nash’s lips caressed River’s neck one more time. “Where can we eat this food I brought?”

River forced himself to pull away. “Let me clean my station real quick and wash my hands. There’s a room in the back with a couch. We can eat back there.”

Nash watched as River pulled out the retractable vacuum hose from beneath his station and sucked up the hair. He tossed a fresh cape across the back of the chair before heading for the sink. With his hands washed, he motioned for Nash to follow. Nash handed a drink to River before grabbing his drink and the bag from the counter where he had abandoned it to hold River. River led the way. The room in the back was mostly used as a peaceful waiting room.

Customers were served wine while sitting in the dimly lit room and listening to soft music. His mom claimed people were willing to wait much longer in a quiet space with wine in their hand. She was right as far as River could tell. It was the most peace a majority of their customers got from their busy daily lives.

River settled on the couch. Nash's wide frame filled the spot beside him, giving River the same feeling Nash's presence always gave him—like he was safe. Like he was home.

"I checked your sandwich before I left the deli. I know how they like to put mayo on the turkey instead of the spicy mustard you like. They got it right."

A smile tugged at the corners of River's mouth as he watched Nash unpack their lunch. He was amazing. Almost too good to be true.

Nash's gaze lifted and collided with River's. He froze. "What?"

River shook his head. "Where did you come from?"

Nash's expression went from slightly perplexed to downright confused. "Um. Down the street."

River's smile turned into a chuckle. "That's not what I meant. You're like the greatest guy I've ever met. Sometimes it hits me all over again that you just landed in my life from nowhere—like we were meant to be." He shook his head as he realized how he sounded. "Sorry. I'm corny."

"I love it," Nash said, stealing a quick kiss. "Let's eat this real quick so we can make out until I need to go back to work."

With a chuckle, River dug into his lunch. He wasn't missing out on any of Nash's kisses. River swore they were magic and solved everything. It was funny how the childlike belief that kisses fixed everything transformed and carried into adulthood in a different way. Further proof Nash was the one, as far as River was concerned. He didn't think there was any way he was wrong about them.

The spa where River worked was in the high-end district. The building was full of stonework and gorgeous. The place screamed money and Nash always looked out of place when he showed up there. He always half expected someone to call the cops as he approached the building, but no one ever did.

Tonight was no different. Nash slipped inside the spa before the woman who worked the front counter could lock him out as she left for the night.

She smiled as he passed her by. “Hey. River is in the back, sanitizing his tools. If you head all the way down the hall, it’s the last door on the left.”

He dipped his chin at her. “Thanks.”

“No problem,” she said with a wink. “Have a great weekend.”

“You too.” He followed her directions down the hall, more than ready to see River. Nash had been thinking about River’s words at lunch all day. It did feel a lot like they were meant to meet. It was possible he needed to stop being so damn scared of losing River and tell him all the things, starting with how much he loved him. Maybe if he said the words, he could ask the questions that burned in his throat.

Nash's steps slowed as River came into view. That bitchy guy, Geoff, who River didn't particularly like for all the right reasons, was there too. They both had their backs to Nash, working side by side.

Geoff's voice reached Nash before he could make his presence known. "What's the story with that guy you're dating?" Nash froze.

River glanced Geoff's way. "What do you mean?"

Geoff didn't respond right away. When he did, he sounded hesitant. "I mean, like, how well do you know him?"

"We've been dating a few months. Why do you ask?" River sounded like he knew exactly why Geoff asked—like Geoff intended to encroach.

"I think he's dangerous," Geoff said fast—like he didn't expect the claim would go over well. Anger had Nash seeing red.

River snorted. "Okay." The disbelief was thick in River's voice. "He's a teddy bear. I don't think he's ever as much as raised his voice at me."

Nash smiled at River's defense of him. It disappeared the instant Geoff opened his mouth again.

"I'm serious, River. You know I've met a lot of men over the years. That one has something in his eyes. You should be careful. That's all I'm trying to say—like if he starts throwing out crazy signals, or starts getting really controlling, you should run. Okay? I don't want to see you get hurt."

Nash had heard enough. He stepped further into the room. "Hey, baby. You ready to go?"

Geoff shot a panicked look Nash's way. Nash held his stare, letting him see that he had heard. Geoff immediately turned away again, but not before Nash saw the fear in his eyes. He should be scared. Fucker. Nash would show him dangerous if he hurt Nash's relationship.

If River noticed, he didn't let on. He scurried across the room to greet Nash. His usual smile was in place. "Hey. I didn't notice the time." He kissed Nash.

Nash focused his full attention on River and let the Geoff thing go for now. "There's no rush.

Finish whatever you need to do. Can I help in some way?"

River motioned toward a nearby chair. "Sit there and look pretty. I've got this."

Nash sat. His eyes stayed glued to River as River moved around the room, gathering his things. His hunger grew by the second as he watched River work. This one was his. He would do anything to keep him. They were perfect together. He forgot about Geoff until the guy moved. Their gazes met and held. The worry etching Geoff's features made Nash wonder how intense he looked while watching River.

Charlotte appeared in the doorway over his shoulder, snagging his attention. "I'm headed out, boys. Oh, hey, Nash." She set her hand on his shoulder. Nash reached up and patted her hand.

He looked up and met her gaze. "Do you need any help out?"

Her smile made the offer worthwhile. "I would love that. Come on." As he stood, she looked River's way. "Text me later and let me know when you two make it home. I love you."

"Love you too, Mom. Be careful going home."

Nash followed her out. She had two boxes of samples to carry out. Nash grabbed both and followed her to her car.

"I haven't had a chance to really talk to you alone," Charlotte said over her shoulder as she unlocked her trunk. "What are your parents like? Maybe we could get together for a get-to-know-each-other gathering or whatever."

Nash put the boxes in the trunk and tried to think of something polite to say. In the end, he went with the truth. After all, he planned to keep River for good. "My dad died when I was little, and my mom is an alcoholic." He turned and met Charlotte's stare. "I recently had to make the hard decision to cut ties with her before she drowned me."

Charlotte pulled a pained face. "I'm so sorry. Actually, I completely understand that. Addiction runs in our family too. I had to make that same tough decision about my dad when I was pregnant with River. He stole a bunch of money from us and I just couldn't take the stress any longer. A big part of me hoped he would get his life together when he realized I was really done with him. Unfortunately, that wasn't the case. He died of an overdose when River was ten."

"I'm sorry to hear that." He really was. There was also a big part of him that hoped his mom would finally see how Mike kept her down. He hoped one day she would wake up sick of the liquor and abuse. Tired of Mike's drug addiction. But really, he knew that day would never come, and he couldn't go down with her. "Sometimes, loving someone isn't enough to save them."

Charlotte sniffed, as if fighting back tears. She smiled, visibly shaking off the memories he had obviously dragged to the surface. "Anyhow, you have us now. I know I can't take anyone's place, but I'm damn glad to have you. It's obvious you really love my son, and that's all I ever wanted for him." She took an audible breath and pushed on. "Truth be told, being a parent is absolutely terrifying. You have no control over what happens. All you can do is pray they end up with someone who loves them as much as you do to blunt life's inevitable disappointments. So you have no idea how grateful I am for you. Your mother should be proud of the son she raised."

Nash was moved. He didn't think anyone had ever been proud of him. "Thank you. River is the best thing that's ever happened to me. I won't take that for granted. I don't have anyone else." Even though he had confessed more than he was comfortable with, Nash didn't regret a thing. He loved River. If he could help it, he wouldn't lose him.

"Well, I'll let you get back in there to him before he thinks I stole you."

Nash chuckled. "I don't know if that's what he'll think. Most likely, he's worrying himself sick that we're exchanging embarrassing stories."

The way Charlotte laughed said she knew he was right. "You should tell him I told you the story of how I found out he likes boys. I won't, but you should tell him I did. He'll die."

Nash laughed but didn't agree or disagree. Instead, he accepted her hug goodbye and headed back inside. He found River now alone where he left him. Nash closed the door behind him and locked it on the sly.

River glanced over his shoulder as he dug capes from the washer and threw them in the dryer. "Did Mom burn your ears with horrible stories about me?"

Without a word, Nash closed the distance between them and molded against River's back. His lips found River's earlobe. His brushed a light kiss across his ear before sinking his teeth in, lightly nipping. River slapped his hands down on the washing machine and held on as Nash reached down and roughly palmed his cock through his jeans. Nash had no mercy in his heart. He held River tight against his chest while getting him hard and sucking his neck. Nash was already rock hard with River's moving against him.

"I want you," Nash said against River's ear. "Are there any cameras in here?"

"No."

At the breathless answer, Nash made quick work of unzipping River's jeans. He shoved his hand inside and rubbed every place he could reach. River whimpered, driving him insane. His gaze desperately shot around the room. A coconut-based oil for hair caught his eye. He reached for it. All sanity had gone. He shoved at River's jeans, uncaring of where they were or what kind of mess they made. He needed River now. Nash set his erection free and coated it with the oil. He urged River's hips back as he bent him over the washer. He was inside River before even a hint of sanity came back to him. His frenzied motions slowed with River's tight heat squeezing him. Even as he rocked inside River, he reached around and played with River's erection. Nash closed his eyes and thrust while stroking River in time. He treated River's cock like he would his own. Nash squeezed and tugged, moving faster as his thrusts increased. He moved closer to the edge, taking River with him. Hot cum coated his fingers as River's body tried sucking him deeper. Everything turned crystal clear in Nash's head as his orgasm hit. This was as close to perfect as he had ever been, and Nash wanted this forever. He would tell

River everything and then beg the man to marry him. He never wanted anyone else.

With his pants around his ankles, cum dripping onto the floor, and no clue how he ended up here, River struggled to catch his breath. One second, he had been finishing his final duties for the day. The next, he was on fire. His mind was a mess. Words crowded his throat and stuck. This was insanity and River loved it. He felt wanted like he never had before. No one had ever fallen on him like they couldn't stand another second of not being inside him. They were a sticky mess. Not to mention, he had been working all day and hadn't showered or prepped in any way. Nash kept kissing every place he could reach like none of that mattered a damn bit to him. To be honest, River didn't care either. Love made him not care about a lot of things.

"Goddamn, baby. I'm not sorry."

River laughed at Nash's breathless claim. "What just happened?"

Nash cupped his jaw and urged River back against his chest. He kissed River's ear. "Your mom told me how she found out you're gay and then I couldn't keep my hands off you."

"Shut up." Even to River's ears, he sounded winded. "She did not."

A sexy rumble of laughter caressed his skin. "No. She didn't. I can't ever keep my hands off you. I don't need an excuse."

"We should clean up so we can go home."

"Agreed. I want to scrub your body in the shower, feed you, and tuck you into bed before holding you all night."

River had to take a breath. His eyes automatically fell closed in pleasure at the picture Nash painted. "Yes. I want that. No work tomorrow. Just us all day long. Damn. I can't wait."

"We should hurry."

As Nash pulled out, reality struck River. "Oh, shit. I didn't think about a condom."

Nash didn't look worried. In fact, he almost looked calculating. "I haven't been with anyone else in a long time and I've tested negative for everything since then."

River nodded. That was okay, then.

Nash still watched him with the same intensity. "Is that okay? I don't plan to let you go, so..."

River's heart melted. He liked the idea of forever. "Yeah. I'm good."

For a moment, River almost thought he saw triumph flash in Nash's eyes, but he turned away too quickly for River to be sure. Nash helped him clean up before fixing River's clothes. It was slightly embarrassing but mostly the sweetest moment River had ever experienced. Then they worked together to quickly finish River's final duties before sneaking out the backdoor without running into Geoff. River was extra thankful for that last part. Even though River had laughed it off at the time, he hated Geoff's accusations. Nash didn't deserve them. While Geoff had always been a bit much for River's tastes, he had gone too far tonight. River was about ninety-eight percent certain Geoff had only said those things because Nash had rejected him. Obviously, if someone wanted River over him, then there had to be something wrong with him. River scrubbed the thought from his mind. He wouldn't let Geoff ruin his night. He had a shower and cuddles to look forward to. Nash brought River's hand to his mouth and kissed it as he drove. River forgot all about Geoff. Nothing else mattered but the love sitting on River's chest. He had met the one.

Chapter Eight

A SATURDAY CONSISTING OF nothing but being kicked back in the recliner with River in his lap all day was Nash's version of utopia. River played a word game on his phone. Nash flipped through the channels and napped some. They kissed a lot. Nash never wanted to move again. Life had never been this peaceful and happy for him.

"What do you want for dinner? I'll get it started."

Nash's lips skimmed River's shoulder. "Hand me my phone and I'll order us something. It's your day off. You shouldn't be catering to me."

River shrugged. "I don't see it that way, but I am pretty comfy," River tacked on with a chuckle. He passed Nash his phone.

After spending a few minutes scrolling through two different food delivery apps, Nash closed them and switched to his camera. He wrapped an arm around River's chest and held the phone out in selfie mode. "Smile, sexy."

River snuggled close and smiled. They eyed the picture together and then took a few more. "We look so happy."

Nash nodded. "That's because we are." His heart rate kicked up. Since they were talking about them, now was as good a time as any to broach the topic of his past, their future, and everything in between. He couldn't keep putting this off. "Speaking of—" The doorbell rang, cutting off his words. His gaze shot to the door. A loud knock sounded.

"Come on, big brother. There's more than one car in the driveway and I can hear the TV. Stop hiding from me and open the door."

River's gaze moved his way. Confusion etched his features. Before he could ask any questions Nash didn't want to answer, Nash heard the doorknob rattle.

"Fine. Looks like I'm picking the lock."

Nash flew to his feet, taking River with him. He had barely tossed River onto the couch before the door flew open. River looked two steps beyond shocked, as he should, but he righted himself and curled his feet underneath himself, getting settled into his new spot.

Jason glanced around the room and stepped inside. "I knew it. You *are* avoiding me." He didn't give Nash time to respond. Jason simply plopped down beside River and dove in—like Nash couldn't and wouldn't throw him out. He looked River's way. "Hey. What's up?"

"Nothing." River dragged the word out, sounding confused as hell.

"This is my friend, River," Nash said, trying to quickly move Jason's attention away from River. "What are you doing here?" With his focus locked on Jason, he still saw River flinch at being called a friend. Nash needed to diffuse this situation as fast as possible.

"Do I need a reason? You're my brother. We're family. You're supposed to want to see me, but I see that's not the case. I've been calling and texting. You're not responding, and I stopped by your work and they said you quit months ago. What the fuck, man? I need to update you on shit with Mom and Dad. How can you just ghost us?" Once again, he didn't give Nash time to think of an answer. He focused on River. "Who are you, again?"

Nash's gaze shot to River. River looked uncomfortable as hell. "Oh. Um, River."

"Cool name," Jason said, immediately dismissing him as unimportant.

River dropped his chin to stare at his knees. "Thanks. It was my mom's childhood crush or something." His feet slipped to the floor. "I should go. This sounds like family stuff."

Nash's chest tightened. Goddamn it.

Jason made a dismissive motion. "It doesn't matter. I'm sure you've already heard everything bad about me from Nash."

With his head down and looking defeated, River moved to the door and stamped into his shoes. He never looked Jason nor Nash's way as he grabbed his keys. "Actually, I didn't even know you existed. Nice to meet you." Without a backward glance, he slipped out the front door before Nash could think of a way to make him stay without showing his hand to Jason.

"I'll be right back," Nash said, rushing after River. He had to make River understand. His family wasn't normal. He didn't have loving parents or supportive siblings. River was as close to sane as Nash had ever felt. He couldn't expose River to their ugliness.

River was already almost to his car, proving how badly he wanted to get away. Nash called out, stopping him. "Please don't leave mad."

River turned. He looked ready to fall apart. His face was pinched while his eyes swam with unshed tears. "I'm not mad. I'm hurt." Nash winced. That was worse, but River didn't stop there. "I feel like..." River pressed his hand to chest. "I feel like I've been heart-jacked."

"Heart-jacked," Nash repeated, sounding confused even to his ears.

River nodded. "There I was, sitting in the car dealership and minding my business, when you came along and stole everything from me. But the thing is, you're *ashamed* of being with me, and it hurts." River pulled a pained face, as if he felt the blows Nash threw his way physically. "I just don't think I can keep doing this. As much as I want to believe that being with you is worth just about anything, I don't know if it's worth my soul, and that's the part of me that feels like it's dying right now being your *friend*." A sad smile touched River's lips and slipped away. He didn't quite meet Nash's stare. "Have a nice life, Nash. I hope you meet someone worth being more than friends with someday. I'm sorry I wasn't the one for you, especially since you were the one for me." River turned away.

Nash couldn't breathe past the pain. "This isn't about you."

"Yet my heart is broken all the same." River didn't look back as he left Nash behind.

Nash had no idea how much time passed before he made his way back inside. Everything hurt. He always lost. It was like he was cursed with a family that was a black hole, swallowing everything good. Jason sat where Nash left him, looking at nothing with his arms crossed over his chest as Nash came back inside. He didn't look Nash's way.

"Couldn't convince him to stay, huh? It seems your cold shoulder isn't reserved for only family."

Nash's everything hurt and he didn't have the mental spoons for this anymore. "What's that supposed to mean?"

Jason's gaze slid his way. He rolled his eyes. "Don't be thick. You obviously hurt that guy's feelings. It's hard as hell loving you. I'm glad to see it's not only family you can't love back."

"I love you." Even Nash heard the hurt in his voice. "You know why I had to cut everyone from my life." As the pain of losing River sank in, Nash's temper rose. His so-called family had broken him down and stolen from him. They had stripped away his innocence and tried to rip away his sanity. He had let them fuck him so bad in the head that he had lost River. Nash had nothing left to give. Nothing left for them to take. "I'm tired, Jason. I'm so goddam exhausted with," he swept his arm wide, "this. Aren't you tired? I want a normal fucking life and I'll never have that as long as my family is in it. I wish that didn't include you. I want you in my life, and I hate to be that dick that says it's me or them, but it's me or them. That guy who just left here, he means everything to me, and as soon as I saw you, I called him just a friend because this family would eat him alive. I hurt him because of you. That's the person this family makes me, and I don't want to be that guy anymore. If you want to be that person, be that person somewhere else, because I'm done."

With a sharp nod and looking everywhere but at Nash, Jason stood. "Yeah. I get that. Thanks for saying it to my face, I guess. I guess that was all I was looking for." He headed for the door. Nash fought the urge to beg him to stay and talk. Nash loved his brother. He didn't want this, but he also didn't want to drown with them anymore. Nobody knew or understood, but Jason fucking knew, and his decision to stay in the middle of it all meant that Nash had to let him go. It hurt worse than he expected.

"I love you," Nash said before Jason could get away. "If you decide you want out, I'll be right here."

Jason kept his gaze averted. His eyes were bloodshot, and he looked like hell. “I won’t tell anyone about River.”

As Jason walked away, Nash wondered if that would be the last words he ever heard from his brother. Nash sat. This recliner was the last place he had been with River. River’s face as he had been tossed aside floated through Nash’s mind. The image of him flinching as Nash called him a friend wouldn’t leave. The sound of River saying he was done wouldn’t stop pressing on Nash’s ears. Everything was gone now. Nash flew to his feet. He pushed the lamp from the end table. As it crashed to the floor, something inside Nash broke. He hadn’t lost his temper in years. Not really. Nash had ground his back teeth to a pulp while holding his tongue and he had given himself migraines trying to stay silent. He should have told River he loved him. Nash should have said he wasn't ashamed, because he wasn't. Not of River. Never of River. Nash's gaze shot around the room. River was gone. He wasn't ever coming back. Nash had destroyed them, the way he did everything, because fear choked him. He pushed the TV off the entertainment center, feeling nothing as it hit the floor. It wasn't enough. Nash opened the coat closet behind the front door and found the baseball bat he kept inside. His gaze skirted the room, searching for what he could destroy next. None of this stuff mattered. He wanted to go after River and beg him to come back, but he couldn't take back who he was on the inside. Nash swung, putting a nice-sized hole in the wall. He didn't feel better. He kept swinging, taking out everything in his path until sweat coated his body. Each breath Nash took heaved in and out. The bat dropped to the floor. He didn't feel better. River was still gone, and Nash had no one else to blame.

Since making it home, River hadn't stopped pacing. His mind raced. He didn't know what to think, and he was scared to feel. Now that he was home, things didn't look the same in hindsight. It was possible he had overreacted. Sometimes, River didn't make the greatest decisions and his mind couldn't be trusted. There were voices in there that weren't Nash's. Nash didn't understand what it was like to be River. River wasn't special. He didn't stand out like Nash. People didn't flirt with River the way they always did Nash. The way Nash had practically thrown River from his lap and then called him a friend, that stuck in River's throat, choking him. Maybe it shouldn't, but that was the first time Nash's actions mimicked the thoughts that plagued River. River wasn't a prize. Maybe this was just what life would be like for him with everyone. Maybe his ex, Jack, had been right. River expected too much for someone with so little to offer.

His doorbell rang, distracting him from his downward spiral. River checked the peephole. He blinked and checked again. The scene didn't change. Jason stood on the other side. A spike of fear went through River. He didn't know this guy. How had Jason found him? The doorbell rang again. River looked out the peephole once more. Jason looked sad. Curiosity won. River opened the door, but he held tight to it, in case he needed to slam the door closed.

Jason gave a small wave. "Hi. Sorry to show up like this."

"How did you know where to find me?" He couldn't imagine Nash telling Jason where River lived.

A self-deprecating smile touched Jason's lips. "Yeah, so, I ran your tag number."

River blinked, trying to wrap his mind around Jason's words. "What?"

To his surprise, the giant and tattooed man on his porch blushed. He scrubbed at the back of his neck, looking guilty. "I guess since you said you didn't know I exist, Nash didn't tell you that we used to memorize people's tags and run them for our dad—my dad—so his buddies could rob houses while people were out. Some lessons you never forget. I took note of your tag number earlier and looked you up when I left Nash's."

River fought to keep up. "So you're here to rob me?"

"No," Jason said, rushing to reassure him. "Sorry. I just want to talk. Did you really not know I exist?"

The hurt in Jason's voice spoke to River's freshly broken heart. He held the door open wider and motioned Jason inside. "I was upset," River admitted as he closed the door behind Jason. "In retrospect, I do recall him saying he had a younger brother and older stepbrothers."

Jason chose the same spot on the couch where Nash always sat. The brothers looked nothing alike. Whereas Nash was dark, Jason was light. Light eyes and hair. He didn't hide his tattoos.

Jason had bad decision written all over him. River got the feeling many people had loved regretting him.

For a moment, Jason inspected the room before focusing those light green eyes on River again. "I see what my brother sees in you. You obviously have a good job." His gaze moved down River's body in a blatantly sexual way that made River want to blush and cover himself. "You're sexy. I can see the appeal."

River didn't budge from his spot by the door. "Should I regret letting you in?"

A smile exploded across Jason's face. It was heart-stopping. He looked sweet and mischievous at the same time. This one had definitely shattered hearts. He was trouble. "You don't have anything to worry about. I may be a bastard, but I've never tried stealing a man from my brother."

River crossed his arms and still refused to budge. He needed to know Jason's intentions. "Since you didn't know he was gay, I'm sure that hasn't been a trial."

Jason snorted. "Just because Nash hasn't said the words to me or let me meet anyone he's ever dated doesn't mean I didn't know he's gay."

With a nod, River gave up and moved to sit on the other end of the couch. "Why are you here?"

Jason was back to looking nervous. He swiped his hands on his thighs. "I didn't mean to fuck things up between you two."

"You didn't do anything wrong." River couldn't let Jason think this was on him. He took a breath and admitted what still sat on his chest, suffocating him. “Nash called me his friend. While we’ve never had many occasions for him to introduce me to anyone, the times we’ve been in a position to be seen together by anyone he knows, he’s driven me away, changed plans so I wouldn’t encounter his work friends, or called me a friend.” He boldly held Jason’s stare. “I won’t be anyone’s secret. If Nash needs to hide, he’ll have to do it without me. I’ve already fought my battle to live my truth. It’s not fair to expect me to hide.”

“It’s not you he’s hiding. It’s everyone else he knows.”

River rolled his eyes at the asinine claim. “I’m the one who got downgraded to a friend, so how does that make sense?”

The way Jason shrugged said he was unbothered by River's open disbelief. "He only knows horrible people. We broke him from having any desire to have anyone in his life. Except you, apparently," he tacked on, sounding sad. Jason shook his head as if moving past something in his mind. "Look, Nash would kill me and then die if he knew I was here, but I have to try to fix a few things before I leave town. He looked devastated when you left, and I can't have that on my soul on top of everything else I've done over the years. So I'm going to do what he never will. I'm going to tell you about our family. You need to know it's not you he's ashamed of, and I don't think you'll know that until you know the hell we survived."

As much as River wanted to know, there was a part of him that didn't. If Nash hadn't said anything, it felt wrong to hear it from Jason. In the end, they were already over, so River might as well learn why he had lost. "Okay."

"First off, we were never kids. Not in my dad's eyes. To him, we were just one more tool he could use to keep his buddies happy. See, he got the money to open his bike shop from less than legal channels. That's the kind of money you never pay back. The interest on it is too high. Basically, he'll have to do whatever he's told for the rest of his life. That meant his boys did too. Nash and I were boosting cars and running tags before most kids learn to read. Many years and atrocities later, Nash got lucky. He got busted and sent to juvie until he turned eighteen. Then he was free. Free of the system and the family. The lucky bastard walked away from all of it. I was the one left behind." Jason fell silent and turned inside himself for a moment, as if trapped in a nightmare only he could see. He cleared his throat and focused on River once more. "Dad has tried several times to drag Nash back in, but he's got no hold on him any longer." A bittersweet smile touched Jason's lips. "You see, he's not the least bit ashamed of you. It's us he's hiding from. He's protecting you from a family that would rip you to shreds. If my dad thought he could get to Nash through you, he wouldn't hesitate."

It was a lot to take in. If he was being honest with himself, if River had known about all this from the beginning, he might not have given Nash a chance. Their lives were just so different. But Nash was such an amazing guy, and River loved him. Jason's story fit better than River wanted to admit. Nash was very protective of him and never treated him like he didn't want to be seen with him unless it was with someone Nash knew. Fuck. Nash was more than just protective. He was kind and amazing. Nash did things River didn't think men did any-more—like opening doors, carrying everything heavy, driving everywhere so River didn't have to, and tucking him in at night. River's eyes stung. He didn't want to lose Nash over a family Nash didn't choose. River needed a minute to think.

"Would you like something to eat?" River had to take care of the brother Nash obviously loved. Maybe Nash's family were awful people, but he hadn't tossed this one out, even though he had broken in. That meant he cared.

Jason looked adorably taken aback by River's offer. "Actually, that would be awesome. I don't know how long it'll take me to get settled when I get to Vegas. So, admittedly, I haven't been eating very often so I can save money."

River flashed him a bright smile. "You're moving to Vegas? That sounds exciting."

Jason nodded. "That's why I stopped by to see Nash. I wanted to let him know I was getting out and leaving town." A sad smile touched his lips. "Who knows? Maybe I'll become someone new. Until then, though, I have to save every dime I can."

"Don't worry," River said, pushing to his feet and heading for the kitchen. "I've got you." He would too. River planned to ply Jason with food and learn all he could about Nash while he could. Then he would plot the best way to beg for Nash's forgiveness, because River had been wrong. If Nash would let him, maybe it was time they were a little more honest with each other. River had at least one thing left to say.

Chapter Nine

WHILE STANDING AT THE front door, Nash played the adult version of head, shoulders, knees, and toes: sanity, keys, wallet, and phone. He still felt so much like a fast-moving train mowed him down that he couldn't get his shit together. His heart screamed for him to get a move on. He needed to go after the other half of his heart. His feet hadn't budged yet. As much as he had known he should have told River all about his past sooner, Nash had been scared shitless. River would likely run for the hills. Now, he already had. Nash had to be honest and pray River took him back. The state of his house already proved how little sanity he had without River. He had stared so long at the picture of them he had taken that his eyes nearly crossed. They were so happy together. They couldn't be over. Nash knew it wasn't normal for people to have this level of obsession. He was scared of what he might do next sometimes. But at the end of the day, he loved River and he couldn't stop trying to be in his life. He had to try.

Nash opened the door. River stood on the other side.

"I was just about to knock," River said while looking adorably nervous. He pulled and twisted at the hem of shirt and shuffled from foot to foot.

In his shock, Nash said the first thing that came to mind. "I didn't think we knocked at each other's houses anymore."

River ignored his claim. "Were you headed out? I could come back later."

Nash shook his head. "I was headed to beg my heart to come back home."

"Oh."

A loud sigh rang through Nash's mind. It could not have been more obvious River didn't realize Nash was talking about him. Nash didn't know if River was really that obtuse or that lacking in confidence. Maybe Nash was the one to blame. He hadn't been as open as he should have been.

"That's you," Nash said, incapable of watching River struggle.

River's expression didn't lighten. He still looked ready to puke. "I don't know why you'd do that. I'm the one who should be apologizing."

Okay. That was unexpected. "What?"

At his question, River's gaze fully latched on to his, and his shoulders visibly squared. "It's not your fault I'm like this. You've done nothing to deserve my lack of faith in us. It's not you at all. I'm just not... ugh," River said, looking ready to stamp his foot. "I'm in love with you and we don't match." Nash blinked at the angrily spoken confession. River didn't give him time to respond. "You're sexy and confident. People flirt with you everywhere we go, because they all see what I already know. You're too hot to be with someone like me, but you are with me for whatever reason, and I worry myself sick you'll figure out someday that you can do better. So, when people come around and you act like we're not together, it's like I've been given proof that everything my ex used to tell me is the truth. No one wants me. I'll always be alone. I shouldn't bother trying to find anyone, because I'm not what men are looking for. But, goddamn, every time I start feeling confident about us, you pretend I'm just a friend or push me away so your family doesn't see me." River took an audible breath, as if physically cutting off the words that poured out. He took another as he focused on Nash. Nash swore he could see the rage bleeding away while River stared at him. "I love you," River repeated, making Nash every bit as happy as the first time. "I'm sorry I left. You are not the problem. My mind is."

First off, Nash craved crushing an ex beneath his boot. River hadn't spoken a word about any exes before this moment, so it hadn't occurred to Nash there might be a reason for River's inability to hear and see Nash's love. Someone had gaslit him and damaged his senses. Right now, though, Nash had bigger fish to fry. "I love you too. You are the sexiest man I've ever known and I'm not the least bit ashamed to be with you. In fact, you shouldn't have wasted your time on me in the first place." Nash pulled a pained face. "You're way out of my league."

River shuffled closer. "Is it okay if we go inside?"

Nash came back to reality and realized he had left River standing on the porch. "Sorry. I didn't mean to make you feel unwelcome." He swallowed. His throat hurt.

River shifted from foot to foot again. He looked worried. "Are you okay? I don't have to come in."

Nash swallowed hard again, trying to work past the pains in his chest. His hands found River's face. He stroked River's jaw and stared into the big blue eyes he loved so much. "I really thought you were done with me this time. You're the one thing I can't lose. You're all I have."

River grabbed Nash's hands and pulled them away from his face. He held tight to them as he stared down at the busted and still trying to bleed knuckles on both of Nash's hands. "What the actual fuck, Nash? What did you do?"

Nash winced. When he spoke, his voice came out sounding every bit as strained as he felt. "I'm sorry. I guess I didn't take losing you very well."

River lifted his gaze to Nash's. Worry swam in his eyes. "What did you do?"

His shoulders heaved as he took a deep breath. Nash moved aside so River could see the room behind him.

River's expression snapped closed as he stepped over the threshold. His head turned from side to side as he took in the destruction. He turned in a circle, eyeing the room. Nash watched him for any signs of finally being pushed too far by Nash's bullshit. River's gaze finally landed on Nash. He didn't blink.

"Well, you know, if you knocked the wall down between the living room and kitchen, this room would be brighter."

A smile tried pulling at Nash's lips, but he couldn't do that. He couldn't let River laugh this off. "Don't do this, River. Don't act like you can't see I'm not normal."

River didn't flinch or back down. "I see you just fine. You are deeply passionate, and it doesn't always come out in the healthiest of ways." He shrugged. "I kind of need that in my life. Without you, I feel invisible and exposed at the same time. I'm not afraid."

Nash closed the door. He held River's stare. "I spent my teenage years living in a juvenile detention center." He had to say it all now. "Mike, my stepdad, he used all us kids to fund his bike shop and his addictions. When I was fourteen, I got busted stealing a car for him. I got locked up until I turned eighteen. When I got out, I didn't immediately fly right. I made more bad decisions and did more jail time. When I was twenty, Mike tried again to pull me into his bullshit. When I refused to let him guilt me into pulling a job for him, he shot Jason in the leg.

When that didn't break me, he realized he no longer controlled me, but that's not completely true. I've been giving Jason money ever since, doing my best to help him out. If he would shoot his own son to hurt me, I can't imagine what he would do to you. I should've told you all of this from the beginning. It wasn't fair for me to let you fall in love with me without knowing who I am. I have a bad temper, and I've made a lot of horrible decisions, but I love you, River. You don't have to worry that will ever change, but I can't let my family find out about you. I also can't let you go on believing that's because I'm ashamed of you. I'm not. You are very literally the only good thing that's ever happened to me."

River stared at Nash with his bottom lip held between his teeth. He worried at it, as if taking it all in. "Do they know where you work now?"

Nash shook his head. "That's one of the reasons I took the job."

"But they obviously still know where you live."

Nash nodded. "I'm kind of stuck on that one, but I told Mom I don't want them coming around anymore."

"You're not stuck," River said, taking him by surprise. "Come live with me and take my last name. I'll keep you safe."

For a full minute, Nash could only blink. Things had taken a twist. "Did you just ask me to marry you?"

River gave him a sharp nod. "Yes, I believe I just did."

River never ceased to shock and amaze him. Nash had gone into this with every intention of asking River to marry him if River took him back, and River had beaten him to the punch. He realized he was taking too long to answer when River's expression faltered. "Yes," Nash said quickly before River could take it back. "I want to marry you."

A shy smile touched River's lips. Nash could practically feel him turning bashful. "Okay." His gaze skirted the room once more. "We should probably clean this up."

Nash's long stride ate up the distance between them. The mess could wait. Nash couldn't. He claimed River's mouth with all the fierceness in his heart. Nash lifted River's feet from the floor in a desperate attempt to hold him closer. River kissed him back, matching Nash's passion stroke for stroke. His legs wrapped around Nash's waist. Nash took River down onto the couch with pieces of drywall trapped beneath him. If River noticed, he didn't complain, and Nash was too far gone to wait. He tore at River's clothes. Even though Nash was hard enough to bend steel with his dick, this wasn't about sex. He had almost lost River, and then he had almost lost himself. Nash just wanted to feel River's skin against his. Once he had River nude, Nash couldn't stop. He open mouth kissed a path down River's body until he had River's cock in his mouth. Pre-cum coated his tongue. Nash sucked and licked while River moaned beneath him.

"Nash." The breathless-sounding whisper of his name on River's lips nearly snapped Nash's mind. He made quick work of the front of his jeans, setting his erection free. Nash stroked his dick while sucking River's. He let River fuck his throat as he pumped faster, getting closer to losing his sanity. River was desperate beneath him, pulling at his hair and scratching his shoulders. When River stiffened beneath him, Nash held his breath. River's entire body jerked. Cum flooded Nash's mouth. The taste of River sent him over the edge. His body shook as he shamelessly shot his load on the couch, uncaring of anything anymore. He still had River. They would be married soon, and River would never get away. Nothing else mattered.

River kissed every bump of Nash's spine as he thoroughly inspected his man's body. He was super unhappy about those busted knuckles. River needed to make sure he didn't have any more injuries. Somewhere between asleep and awake, and spread nude across the bed, Nash tolerated his ministrations.

"Where did you get this scar?" River traced the long gash across Nash's back with his tongue so Nash would know which scar he meant.

"Mike threw me through a glass door when I was ten because I didn't understand my math homework and didn't want to do it." The words came out slurred as Nash moved closer to being asleep. River's eyes burned. He had only been given the slightest glimpse into a nightmarish childhood and River wanted to make it disappear. He loved Nash. It was unfair that he had suffered what no child should.

"I love you," River whispered against his skin, in case he had finally drifted off. River was exhausted too, but he was too excited to sleep. He still couldn't believe he had asked Nash to marry him and that Nash had said yes. River hadn't planned to do any such thing. Some form of crazy protectiveness had risen in his chest once Nash told him everything. River had to take him away from the people who hurt him. Give him a new life.

Nash suddenly rolled, snagged River around the waist, and tucked him beneath his body in one quick motion. River chuckled over his new circumstances—wrapped in a cocoon of huge man. "All you had to do was tell me stop. I'll let you sleep."

"Shush. I want to hold you."

River pressed his lips together, trying not to say anything else, but he couldn't stop smiling. "We should elope."

"Your mom would die, and then kill you, and then die again."

That was true. "Oooh, then we should have a wedding on the beach."

"River." River pressed his lips together again at the scolding in Nash's voice. "I love you," Nash added, making River's shoulders relax.

"I love you too."

"You're not going to sleep, are you?"

"Sorry."

"Don't apologize."

“Sorry,” River repeated without thought.

A loud sigh escaped Nash a half second before his body came down full weight upon River. His mouth covered River’s before River could complain about his inability to breathe. He loved the way Nash kissed. Everything the man did made River feel cherished. Then Nash’s hips rolled. He leaned away just enough to press his forehead against River’s, and he held River’s stare. Nash didn’t look away as he rocked again, using the friction between their bodies to hold River’s attention.

“If you won’t sleep, then tell me what you fantasize about when you’re alone.”

A hot blush exploded through River’s cheeks at the question. “Hard pass.”

The sexiest and most evil rumble of laughter vibrated from Nash's chest. "You can do this, gorgeous." He kept moving against River, making his body burn. "I'm always fantasizing about you. In the shower. At work. There's no place I don't want you."

"I think about the way you held me that first night," River said fast before he could change his mind.

Nash went still. He didn't look away. River swore he held his breath. "And?"

River swallowed. "And I'm in your arms again, except you're watching me instead of a movie. You look hungry—like you do now. I'm wearing the shorts you like. The thin cotton ones." River swore Nash's cock twitched and a drop of pre-cum leaked onto his stomach. He couldn't stop now. "Except I don't have on anything underneath. You make me touch myself while you watch. So, I have my hand inside my shorts, trying to come while you stare at me."

"Goddamn," Nash breathed, sounding on the edge of orgasm. "I want that."

A smile exploded across River's face. "Maybe tomorrow."

With a growl, Nash reclaimed River's mouth. The way he took no mercy let River know he was in for a long night. River couldn't wait. This was the other half of his soul. He needed to be pieced back together.

Chapter Ten

THE VISION OF RIVER, covered in flecks of plaster and paint from helping Nash repair the drywall, had Nash silently vowing to never be so dumb again. While River was adorable wearing one of Nash's work shirts, Nash hated that River wouldn't let him clean up the mess alone. River deserved better than this.

With the front door standing wide open, letting fresh air in and the paint fumes out, Detective Ranking got the drop on them. "Spring cleaning for the fall, huh?"

Nash spun, ready to defend River from an intruder. His ire fell away at the sight of the now elderly cop who had helped him many years ago to break from his family. He flashed Craig a welcoming smile and crossed the room to shake the man's hand. "Actually, we're getting the place ready to put on the market."

Craig's eyebrows rose. "We?"

Nash nodded toward where River stood half hidden by the open front door, working to get some paint from his face before anyone saw him. "My fiancé and I," Nash clarified.

Craig's gaze slid River's way. He stepped closer and extended his hand. "Detective Craig Ranking."

"River Yearly," River said, accepting his handshake, openly trying not to smear Craig with paint.

Craig paused, as if slightly taken aback. His gaze moved over River's face, as if seeing something only he knew. "You're not by any chance kin to Todd Yearly, are you? I swear you look just like him."

River's smile brightened. "That's my dad."

"Oh, wow," Craig said, looking shocked. "Your dad is a great guy. We go way back. He heads up the fundraiser every year for the precinct's Thanksgiving community give-back program."

River nodded. "I've helped out a few times."

Craig's smile grew. Nash didn't like the way Craig looked at River. "I thought you looked like a face I'd seen before." Before Nash could growl and beat his chest, Craig was focused on him once more, looking serious again. "I hate to bring this to your door like this, Nash, since I know you've worked hard to get away from your family."

"But," Nash said, hoping Craig got to the point of his visit sometime today.

"But Mike was found dead at his shop last night."

Nash was unfazed. "I'm guessing it wasn't a heart attack."

Craig dipped his chin. "Shot in the head."

"Shocker." At his heartless tone, River's eyebrows rose, but he didn't say anything. Nash wasn't taking it back. River didn't know. The world would be a better place without Mike.

Craig winced. "I really hate to ask, but where were you yesterday between four and six?"

Nash pulled a face. "You know damn well it was nowhere near that piece of shit."

"He was here with me," River said. Nash ground his back teeth. River had not been with him during those hours. Those were damn near the exact hours River hadn't been there. Nash didn't want River lying for him. "We were home all day."

Craig nodded, taking River's word as gospel. His gaze slid back Nash's way. "What about Jason? Do you know where he was yesterday?"

"He was here too," River lied, making Nash half insane. He couldn't let River end up in jail for Jason. Before Nash could intervene, River dug a deeper hole. "We had kind of a going-away thing. Just the three of us. Jason got a job in Vegas, and yesterday was his last day in town. He got here around noon and left at like," he stared at Nash, looking as if he truly tried to recall what time Jason left, "eight or nine, I think."

Goddamn. Nash believed him and he knew it was a lie. Craig looked fucking enamored. When he looked Nash's way again, Nash swore the guy had to tear his stare away from River. "Well, I'm glad to know you boys were nowhere near the scene. There aren't any security cameras in or around the shop and there are countless sets of fingerprints all over the place that are basically useless, considering customers are in and out of there all day. Can you think of anyone who might have it out for Mike?"

Nash snorted.

"That's what I thought," Craig said, sounding tired. "One last question. When is the wedding?"

"We're still working on a set date, but soon," Nash said as River came to stand beneath his arm.

River held on to Nash's waist even as he gave Craig all his attention. "You'll have to let me know where we can send an invitation."

To Nash's surprise, a smile exploded across Craig's face. "Nash knows how to reach me. I have to say, this is a good thing. It warms my old heart to see Nash settled down like this, and finally getting the good, respectable family he deserves."

River and Craig exchanged more pleasantries as River walked the man to the door. Nash bit his tongue so hard, he tasted blood. He stayed that way until Craig backed from the driveway. Then his breath left him in a whoosh as he focused his full attention on River. “Why did you just lie to him like that? You could go to jail for lying to the police.”

River shrugged, looking completely unfazed. “I’m not worried. You didn’t kill him.”

Nash nearly blacked out in his panic. “I don’t mean me. Why did you lie for Jason? There’s a very real possibility he did it, baby. Jason is completely capable of having done it.”

River chewed his bottom lip and twisted the hem of his shirt, looking guilty. “Um, if he did, then he didn’t kill the guy between four and six. He was with me.”

Nash's mind blanked. "I'm sorry. Did you just say Jason was with you?"

River pulled a pained face. "I should've told you yesterday, but things were kind of nuts. He said he memorized my tag number and ran it when he left here. That's how he found me. He wanted to know if I really never knew about him. I made him dinner, and he told me about his plans to move to Vegas. Someone named Soupy, and I really hope I got that name wrong, got him a job customizing bikes there. A legit job. He said he was done with the family and needed to be done with this town." River shrugged. "And since you were done with him, he had nothing left holding him here." Nash wanted to rage at River for letting Jason into his life. Anything could have happened to him, but there was still a small part of Nash that trusted

Jason, and River looked so nervous. He really looked like Nash could get angry with him. River didn't give him time to voice his fears. "Are you okay?" River asked, shuffling closer. He took Nash's hands, his eyes filled with concern. "I know you hated Mike, but he still raised you. It's okay if you feel a little something about him being... you know."

He was sweet. He couldn't even say Mike was murdered. Nash brushed the back of his knuckles across River's jaw. "Will you think I'm terrible if I say I saw this coming? Honestly, I can't believe he made it this long. He was a bad person. People like him always come to a bad end."

River blew out a breath, blowing a strand of hair out his eyes. "Okay. If the shock wears off and you want to talk about it, I'm here."

Nash was a lucky bastard. He would never forget it. "I wonder how my mom's taking this?"

River rubbed Nash's arms. "We can go check on her, if you'd like."

With a shake of his head, Nash shook off the hint of concern that had tried sneaking in. "No. That was the part of me that wished I had a good mom talking. I can't let this be the thing that drags me back down their black hole."

River nodded. "Whatever you decide, I'll be right there with you."

Nash tugged River into his arms and hugged him against his chest. Every time he thought he couldn't get luckier, River did something else that made Nash realize how blessed he was for having met River. He didn't say anything and wouldn't, but Nash's heart did hurt. Not for

Mike. Mike had that shit coming for a long time. Nash's heart broke over Jason. His baby brother had finally gotten out and Nash had cut him from his life before he could hear Jason say the words.

He kissed River's forehead. "So someone named Soupy got my brother a job, huh?"

River chuckled. "Yeah. He seemed pretty excited about a fresh start. I gave him my cellphone number so he could text me his new address once he gets settled. For now, he's staying with the owner of the shop until he can find a more permanent place. I bet it's super expensive to live there."

"I imagine so." Nash fought the urge to open his pay app and send Jason money. He needed to hang on to his savings for once. Nash had a wedding to pay for soon. He had to let Jason sink or swim all on his own. “When are we getting married?” Nash asked, determined to move past the ugliness of the day.

River bit his lip and Nash fought a smile. He knew whatever adorable suggestion came from such a nervous look was something he would do, no matter what River asked of him. “I thought maybe we could wait a month or two so we can get everything together and Jason can get settled in Vegas. Then, maybe, we can send Jason the money to come back for the weekend so he can attend. Of course, I want you to move in right away. You can’t stay here.”

Nash’s throat swelled over River wanting to send Jason money. “I wish you saw what I see when I look at you. I’ve never met anymore more beautiful inside and out. You don’t realize how loved you are, but I do, and I won’t fail you.”

River's gaze never wavered from holding Nash's stare. "I have complete faith in us." River's expression matched his words. It was obvious he had zero doubts. Nash was ready to make him proud. He was ready to spend the rest of his life with this man.

"I love you."

River smiled. "I love you too."

He did. Nash could see it in River's eyes, and that was the biggest miracle Nash had ever witnessed. He never dreamed that a simple offer of free labor would change his life forever. Nash couldn't be more grateful that it had.

Keep an eye out for the next Messy Hearts, *Soul-Wrecked.*

Please consider clicking this link and leaving a review, https://www.amazon.com/review/crea

te-review?asin=B082FQYHLG. Reviews really help with a book's visibility, which ensures I can continue writing. Thank you, Charity.

About the Author

CHARITY PARKERSON IS AN award winning and multi-published author with several companies. Born with no filter from her brain to her mouth, she decided to take this odd quirk and insert it in her characters.

*Eight-time Readers' Favorite Award Winner

*2015 Passionate Plume Award Finalist

*2013 Reviewers' Choice Award Winner

*2012 ARRA Finalist for Favorite Paranormal Romance

*Five-time winner of The Mistress of the Dark-path

Connect with her online:

--Join my street team: facebook.com/TeamCharityParkerson

--Website: charityparkerson.com --Facebook: facebook.com/authorCharityParkerson facebook.com/TheMenofSin--Twitter: twitter.com/CharityParkerso

www.ingramcontent.com/pod-product-compliance
Lightning Source LLC
Chambersburg PA
CBHW060151180626
46813CB00007B/2699